Absolution

Dreams lost, dreams found... absolution.

S. Anne Gardner

Affinity
eBook Press
NZ

Absolution
© S. Anne Gardner 2013

First Edition

Affinity E-Book Press NZ LTD
Canterbury, New Zealand

ISBN: 978-1-927282-20-5

Editor: Ruth Stanley
Cover Design: Helen Hayes
Photo Credit: Edson Campos Behind Blue Eyes
             ArtPicsOnFacebook@Edoson Campos

Acknowledgements

Inspiration comes to the writer in so many forms, through the passages of their own lives, the vast pages of read works and finally the imagination. But, most important inspiration comes from the people in one's life.

I find so much beauty in the everyday with the woman that I love. The beauty that she inspires with grace and generosity elevates every aspect of my life.

My sons are the spheres that make my world a living and miraculous thing and for which I am forever changed.

Melinda, I thank you for the clarity that you have guided me to. I cannot tell you how it has enhanced my life. Thank you.

Ruth thank you for the editing of this book; I am fortunate to have worked with you on this project. With your understanding of my writing style, this work has become a greater story.

Belinda you are my Spanish language guru. I could not survive without your knowledge of accents and the laughter of some of my spelling at times. Thank you my friend.

Mel and Julie I am so happy to be a part of such an incredible publishing house. From the beginning, you two have been a joy to work with.

I want to thank all the fans for their emails and good wishes. You all have always been so loyal and for you this book is also written.

Dedication

For my loves and the miracles of my life…
Lisa, Jose IV, Christian, Lorenz and Alexander, without you I would have no meaning and no purpose.
Because of you I live and love… and dream.

By S. Anne Gardner

In the Silence of the Unspoken
An Affair of Love
The Very Thought of You
Till There Was You

Table of Contents

Prologue

I go back to the first moment—the first thought, the first step to a plan that was just a ruse. The only person I truly deceived was myself. It had all seemed so simple, so clear…

I close my eyes and all I see is her face. She has become all-consuming inside me. I am filled with this sweet sense of peace and tenderness to the point of tears. My skin feels the warmth of her skin, the silkiness of it. It is more than just wanting her; she fills me with all the wants of a life having only just begun. How could I think I could run from her, leave her behind me and try to live without her? Almost from the beginning of the thought, of creating a life without her I knew that it would never be possible. This last thought saddened me beyond all else.

A tear escapes and gently rolls down my cheek as I give myself to the first moment and all that inevitably must follow…so much confusion, so much anger, so much pain, so much passion.

No, so much love…

Chapter One

AP WIRE…NEWS FLASH HEADLINES

April 20, 1985 9:15am

TRAGIC ACCIDENT-CAR GOES OVER CLIFF

ALCALAS—RELATIONS TO THE SPANISH
CROWN

WHOLE FAMILY KILLED

✝

Carlotta and Stefan Alcalá had looked like the
perfect couple. Like golden gods with their youth,
good looks and all the trappings that wealth provided.
They led a fairytale life, according to onlookers, until
the day of that horrible accident that ended their lives.
People talked and the media speculated about how
awful it had all been, that the car had gone over the
cliff. The couple had been so full of life; such a
shame. Carlotta and Stefan were both so young and
attractive. They both came from old, well-known
Spanish families and both were related to the Spanish
Crown. Carlotta and Stefan were the epitome of

perfection in every way but the fairytale ended with their tragic death.

Carlotta and Stefan had two beautiful little girls and initially it was believed that both children were in the car. However, the day after the accident, the newspapers reported that only the youngest of the little girls had been in the car with the young Alcalá couple. The older child, Cristina Alcalá, was spared because she had stayed at home with Mrs. Alcalá's mother. So much grief was felt for the poor little girl, Cristina Isabel Alcalá. She had lost her whole family, and in a few seconds her life changed forever.

Photos of the funeral appeared in almost every newspaper in Spain, depicting a stoic child with a majestic elder lady dressed elegantly in mourning, standing along with the Spanish Royal family.

Cristina Alcalá stood next to her maternal grandmother at the gravesite. Her photo was immortalized in the hearts of the nation as she lay down a white rose on the small casket of her baby sister while King Juan Carlos's white-gloved hand held her little hand in his.

A few days after this photo was shared with most newspapers around the world the scandalous details began to emerge. Cristina Isabel Alcalá was taken out of the country by her grandmother immediately.

†

June 2011

"Grandmama, I have to do this," I told her again and again, trying to make her understand and yet knowing she never would.

"*¿Por qué?*" Why, she wanted to know, frustration clearly showing in her face.

"I need to know. I need to finally put this behind me. I won't be able to go on with my life if I don't fully understand my past." My grandmother was a strong woman and she was stubborn, but so was I. We both stood firmly on opposite sides of the line we'd drawn in the sand till she finally turned and walked away slowly before turning to look at me again.

"*¿Por qué sigues hablando en inglés?*" she asked and her voice suddenly sounded sad and filled with the knowledge that she would not be able to change the decision I had made.

"I'm speaking in English because I'm going to be speaking it for a long, long time," was my weary response. I felt tired of this same argument. Weary of the same questions that had plagued and tormented me my whole life. I didn't want to wake up screaming with fear in the middle of the night anymore. I was going to find my answers no matter what I had to do to get them.

I had always been Grandmama's soft spot. She had loved and pampered me like a china doll my whole life, seeming to fear that somehow I might be dropped and would shatter to a million pieces. After my parents died she protected me and tyrannically controlled all around me. She had granted my every desire and all that surrounded me was beauty, creating a life of peace, music, and a garden of colors that filled every aspect of my life with fragrances that filled all the senses. She was not going to allow anything to touch her beloved granddaughter. I was all she had left of her family. With her I had been happy. We had traveled all over the world for many years until finally we went back home to Spain and in that luscious and vibrant countryside I thrived and the past had seemed like another lifetime.

As I got older I realized that Grandmama had forbidden any talk of my parents' death around me. No one was allowed to speak of it. I had gotten close to a few of my nannies and one by one they had all disappeared when at one point or another some tidbits about my parents escaped their lips. She wanted to spare me the pain she said, but the harder she tried to protect me from the details the harder I tried to find out what had happened to them. My memory was incomplete; I yearned to fill the empty blanks. I needed answers and if she was not going to provide them I would go and find them for myself. I simply changed my tactics but always planned one way or another to find out more.

What I could recall of those days before the accident was hazy at best. I had been old enough to remember at least something, but I did not. A doctor told Grandmama that the shock had probably blocked my memory; that sometimes that happened. Sometimes people's mind blanked out memories that were simply too painful to endure, he said. Oddly enough what I remember the most of that day at the doctor's visit was that my grandmama said that she was glad. I still remember that look of relief and that look stayed locked in my mind forever. I never understood that. Why would she want me to forget? Most of all I needed to know why I had lost my sister and why was it such a secret? In retrospect I don't know if that was the only reason, all I knew was that the truth—my truth and my destiny—were in the details that my mind had simply just chosen to forget.

One memory that was intact from that time was the day my mother and father brought María home from the hospital. She was so sweet, so small. I loved her from the very first moment. I remember touching her with my finger and her little hand holding on to me. I loved her with all the goodness inside me. She was truly the only thing that had been mine. As we grew older, we became inseparable. We were dependent on one another. In retrospect, I now know she was the only person that I loved and that loved me back just as much. There was no agenda, I always felt in some ways she was the innocence inside me; that thought never made any sense and it made my head hurt. She had been the only truly good thing in my life.

Mother and Father were never in the nursery much; they traveled a lot, gallivanting all over the world without a thought about their children. I don't know why I felt such animosity over parents I didn't remember. Something inside me knew that loneliness had been a natural part of life. My sister and I were all we had. During those years while we were growing up we clung to one another during the good and the bad. We held each other during the nightmares and the darkness of nights that were not always kind. Having María meant not being alone anymore. I loved her. I loved her so very much. I would have died for her. Many times I wish I had died instead of her.

When Grandmama told me that she had gone to heaven, a part of me just froze. María was with God Grandmama had said. I also recall that from that moment on I believed in nothing. How could a God that was supposed to love take from me the one thing I loved? Something inside me just turned off and I didn't say anything at all. I just stayed quiet. It was a year before I spoke a single word again. I chose to just detach. I chose to not be one with a world that had ripped from me all that mattered, and I chose when I was willing to be one with it again.

After being taken to many doctors, I eventually did speak. I spoke when I was ready. During that time I lived and listened. I processed and I breathed. That was all I found necessary. Although I seemingly acted like most children, I have never felt whole, not really, not ever. She knew. Somehow my grandmama always knew that there was something asleep inside me. She would sometimes just stare at me when she thought I wasn't looking, her eyes possessed with such sadness. I wish she had told me; I wish she had told me so that I could have planned. Perhaps it might all have been different. Perhaps I might have been able to change it all. But, I am just guessing. If given the choice even now I can't honestly say that I would have done anything differently. The one thing that I could have changed I would not…even now. Even after all this pain and all this sadness, this despair growing inside me is like some dark cloud that is about to drown me. I love her, oh dear God, all I feel is this all-encompassing love for her.

My memories before the accident were incomplete. I needed to find a reason why I had lost María. As time passed, my obsession with finding out why my sister had died became all that I thought about. She had been only five when she died in the car with my mother and father. Somehow that part of my life, which I could not remember, ruled my life. Something had happened. If not, then why the mystery I kept telling myself over and over again. Why could I not just move on and let go? Why couldn't I remember? Now I say to myself at times when I am weary why could I not forget?

I began to notice, as I got older, that my grandmother became very agitated as my interest in finding out how and why María had died grew more important to me. Because of this I learned to control my curiosity. I asked fewer questions. But as the years passed, my need to know became paramount to the point that I could no longer hide or keep secret my desire to know the truth. And one day I knew I could not go on without knowing. That day, life led me to my destiny.

Shaking myself out of my reverie, I said, *"Abuela, tengo que ir y usted lo sabe."* I told my grandmother that I needed to go the United States.

At this declaration from me she suddenly looked very tired. She nodded her head, accepting the finality of my decision as she walked away. She looked so old and defeated that a part of me wished that I would let the subject simply fade into the past.

I was the only family she had left and her health had not been good for the past year. She had begun to look frail. I had noticed the slowness of her walk and the softness that was almost unbearable to notice in her eyes when she looked at me. It was as if she had begun to say her goodbyes to me. But nothing could have stopped me from going to the United States. The accident had been there. The answers were there too. And there is where I had to be.

Chapter Two

I got to New York on a cold winter's day in the month of February. The city was dark, yet all the lights made it shine like a magical place. The city oozed of wealth, poverty, beauty, and danger. The store windows were dressed in fineries and within a few more blocks the darkness of a wolves' den also resided. It was heaven and it was hell. Oddly enough I felt at home. A part of me was looking for heaven and a part of me knew that if heaven existed so did hell.

I established myself in a suite at the Waldorf Hotel. I made myself at home there. And I began to live a life on borrowed time. Because somehow, even then, I knew the years that I had spent until now were only a preliminary time until my life would really begin.

After a few weeks of settling in I began to do my research. I looked through old newspaper clippings. I looked through police reports, and I hired someone to dig through all else I might not be able to find out on my own. I had placed myself on a course from which there was no going back. And a part of me knew that this is where I had always been meant to be.

I made use of my acquaintance with two friends, Elena and Alfonso, who lived in New York City. They were the first step to the life that I was meant to live. Through them the door opened and I finally began to breathe.

Funny the things we become aware of. I had not realized that until I first heard her name—or rather saw it on paper during my research. At that moment something inside me long dead came back to life again.

So when I got a call from Elena to join them at a party they were attending I was not very interested…until she told me whose party it was. A skip of breath and a part of me froze. She asked again and finally my voice came back to me. I accepted the invitation. After the call, I sat without moving for what seemed like a century. When I got up I walked into my closet and began to prepare for the beginning. Finally, my life was truly going to begin.

It was a noisy party, festive and every detail had been seen to. But I had come to this party with one objective in mind: to meet Annais D'Autremont.

The party dragged on. And polite conversation and playboys with their agendas had begun to annoy me. As time passed I found myself becoming melancholy. A part of me felt so lonely in the midst of a crowded room. I had been in New York only a few months and so far my search had been going badly. Or I should say, it had not been going fast enough for me. But, I had found something a few weeks ago. I had a name, Annais D'Autremont, and hopefully, after tonight, I would have a face to go with the name.

Even though I had to keep searching I began to tire and I was homesick. I missed Spain and my grandmother. My health had also become a concern. I had begun to use my inhaler more often than in the last few years that I had lived in Spain. I had known that a change of weather or even environment might cause my asthma to present itself more often. And I missed grandmama. I missed the safety of her. She was the only family I had left and my leaving wasn't exactly a pleasant memory. We argued endlessly about whether I should come or not, but I would not be talked out of it. Nothing and no one could have stopped me. However, guilt began to plague me. Each time I spoke with her on the phone I knew her health was failing. I knew she was ill. I knew I might lose the one person I had who loved me. But not even knowing that did I stop to think of her. And when my mind was clear I knew that I should have cared more. I should have loved her more. I should have stayed safe in Spain with her.

I had come to the party with Elena and Alfonso, who had been introduced to me in Spain two years before. Elena was the granddaughter of one of my grandmother's old friends.

As soon as I knew they were living in the United States, my interest in them grew. To tell the truth, if not for this fact, I would not have pursued their friendship. They were nice enough, but they were a couple and sometimes it felt odd spending time with them. Alfonso tended to be too friendly sometimes and that was a problem I didn't need.

I made excuses as to why I couldn't see them very often after arriving in the US, but when Elena called about this party I accepted the invitation immediately. The party was being hosted by the person whose name made all the bells inside my head go off. Her name had at first appeared in a newspaper article that I was reading about my parents. Then I began to notice how it had appeared in a number of other places. I began to put the dots together and she was the one common denominator in it all.

An hour later, the party, packed with the who's who of New York City, was going strong. I aimlessly walked around. Elena and Alfonso were doing their own socializing and had forgotten all about me. I was bored. As of yet I had not found the elusive Annais D'Autremont. I had to find the object of my obsession before leaving. Since I had found her name it was all I thought of. I needed to know. Something inside me drove me on. Sometimes all I could feel was the need to know. Why? What had I forgotten that haunted me even years later? In that piece of my life were all the answers that I needed in order to go on living. Suddenly I was filled with a sense of anticipation, the kind where all your hair stands up all over your body and you are filled with a sense of awakening.

I began to drift around the party again, just walking around listening to different conversations, not engaging in any. I felt someone watching me. I turned and started scanning the room, surprised when my eyes locked with hers. Quite suddenly something rattled inside me. I looked away quickly. Something in this woman's eyes had made me uncomfortable. I had been shaken to my very core. But, like the moth to the fire, I could not resist the allure of the flame.

I found myself looking around the room several times during the remainder of the night and I would always stop as soon as my eyes found her.

She was beautiful, seeming to glide within the room. She was truly exquisite. Immaculately dressed and as she spoke she seemed to mesmerize the people around her. I could see the web she spun around them as she spoke. I could not control the smile that appeared on my lips. You could see men drooling over her as she spun her web of charm and seduction. Because that is what it was, seduction. She played with them all. She liked the reactions, and as our eyes met once more there was a moment of recognition— she knew I could see her game and she smiled back at me. I walked in another direction to put distance between those eyes and myself. I was alive. Every part of me was alive. I could neither run nor stop moving. My heart was beating so fast. My heart, so long, so long it had waited to beat.

Along with the excitement I was also filled with the magic—the magic of breathing and feeling. Suddenly I noticed everything. I found myself noticing the view of New York City from the living room window. I noticed the colors, the sounds and the lights. All the lights in the world had been turned on.

It was such a beautiful night that I decided to go out to the balcony before I started looking for my friends again, and I was filled with an excitement that

I needed to somehow get a hold of. The breeze on the balcony was delicious. It was a warm breeze but it cooled and caressed your skin as it traveled. Indian summer they called a day and night like today. The city looked so beautiful from up here. I raised my face up and closed my eyes as I let the breeze caress my body. I heard a noise from the shadows and my eyes came upon two forms embraced in a passionate kiss. I felt like an intruder. Something about the two figures kept me staring, unable to look away.

You shouldn't be here a voice inside me kept repeating, but I could not move. I heard whispering and a woman emerged from the shadows and, after straightening her dress and running her fingers through her hair, walked back into the party. She hadn't noticed me standing there as she made her way back inside. My breathing seemed to come slowly.

My gaze returned to the darkness and I was met by those same eyes that had met mine over and over again that night. She just stood there looking at me from the shadows. I could only look back. Something inside me switched on and self-preservation screamed *run*! But I could not. I did not want to. I took a deep breath and slowly my chest began to rise and fall—expectant but not sure exactly why.

I felt embarrassment wash over me and, although it was dark and she could not have seen me blush, I realized she knew I had. I knew when her mouth smiled seductively at me. I stood motionless for a moment and then, when she started walking toward me I ran past her and hurried back inside. I had come upon a situation I wanted no part of, something inside me screamed. And yet, I had not escaped when I should have. I had stayed. I had watched. I was unable to not watch.

As I stepped inside I looked around the room frantically but found no sight of Elena and Alfonso.

"I promise I don't bite," I heard a soft voice whisper behind me and I turned toward it slowly. I felt like the whole world was moving in slow motion and a part of me drowned in the mere look of her.

She stood barely a foot away from me. Her perfume filled my senses and up close she was more beautiful to me than she had seemed before. I just stared not knowing exactly what to say. No words would come. I, like so many others that night, was caught in the spell she weaved. I stared, motionless, and then ever so slowly and yet with the weight of a lifetime a movement like from a timepiece turned and my life began again. Like something long dead my heart began to beat.

She put out her hand and said, "My name is Francesca."

I reached out for her. And as I felt the warmth of that first touch the cold inside began to subside and a flame long dead had its rebirth.

She held my hand a moment and just as quickly released it. "Are you going to tell me yours?" she asked teasingly.

I stared a bit longer then suddenly I shook my head and smiled at her.

"Cristina...I'm Cristina," I said, feeling rather foolish. After all, this woman's life was none of my business. She started talking of things in general and I found myself mesmerized by her charm, just as all others had been.

She had the knack of putting people at ease and words began to flow between us. I found myself enjoying my conversation with her. I was relaxed, and for the first time that night I found myself enjoying the party. She was so easy to talk to and I found myself feeling a sense of unguarded freedom that I had not enjoyed in years. When she laughed it was like music; magical notes floated between us and the sound of it began to fill my senses. Soon I was her prisoner just as all the others before me. I felt like the moth again drawn in by the flame. Perhaps through Francesca I could meet the person I was looking for I told myself. I don't know why I made excuses for enjoying her company, how could I not be enticed by her?

We spoke for about an hour while sitting on a large white sofa in one of the side rooms, away from where the party was in its fullest. I had not found anyone in all the time that I had been in New York that I felt so comfortable talking to. My agenda for attending the party seemed to have escaped me with her. There was something soothing and familiar about being with her that I admit I found delicious to all my senses. I forgot all about the incident on the veranda and just allowed myself to enjoy her company. She was like a breath of fresh air that entered my lungs, and I took a deep breath that filled all of me. It was as if with her I had begun to breathe again.

"I've never seen you at one of my parties," she said as she looked around the room, her lips taking a sip from her champagne flute. Every movement seemed to mesmerize me. Suddenly the jolt of her words shocked my system and I felt my world begin to shake.

My eyes flew to her face. "Your party?" I asked, my eyes looking away for a moment before meeting hers again.

"Yes," she said softly, turning to look at me.

"You're Annais D'Autremont?" I asked, unable to hide my surprise.

It only took a moment before I recovered. "You've caught me. I crashed your party with my friends," I said to her with an embarrassed smile. I had made it a point to meet her; that was the reason I had come to this party and now I felt such cold come over every part of me.

"Don't be silly, I'm glad you came," she said gracefully, looking at me in curiosity.

After a few minutes of awkward conversation between us, Alfonso and Elena finally appeared.

"Ah, Annais, finally we get you to ourselves. I see you've met Cristina," Elena said as she and Alfonso walked over to us.

"Yes, we've been talking a good while now," she said with a smile as her hand briefly touched my knee.

Elena and Alfonso joined us and the conversation became a polite exchange of gossip of this person or that. I realized at that moment that she had told me her name was Francesca and yet they all called her Annais. I found this odd. I liked her as Francesca.

When we decided it was time to take our leave, she invited me in particular to lunch and shopping the next day. I agreed to meet her. She then turned politely to Elena and Alfonso and said good-bye to them, then turned to me and kissed me lightly on the cheek. Used to this behavior, as it was natural in Europe, I returned her kiss. As my lips touched her cheek I felt her breath skip. I realized immediately it had been a mistake when I saw her reaction. She then took my hand in hers, holding it a little too long. Her eyes searched mine for a moment. Then she released my hand slowly and smiled. Her veil of calm and gracious good manners was in place once again.

"I'll see you tomorrow, Cristina," she said softly.

I slowly pulled my hand out of hers. It all made me feel surreal for some reason. I was walking toward the door when she spoke again.

"Cristina, your last name? I'm supposed to meet you tomorrow and I don't even know your last name." Her smile and her eyes searched my face with such softness that it took my breath away.

"Alcalá, Cristina Alcalá," I finally answered.

I saw a moment of recognition in her eyes and at that moment I felt our connection break but she quickly masked her thoughts. I felt more than saw the separation between us. I had been right, I told myself.

She knew something. I had to know what it was. This is the closest I had ever gotten to my past. And my excitement got the better of me. I could not hide it.

"Do you know my family?" I asked her directly. After a moment she nodded, her face and her eyes searched mine with newfound interest.

"Perhaps you knew my parents?" I asked. "They were Carlotta and Stefan Alcalá." Her face went pale as I finished. "You knew them, didn't you?" She just stared at me without saying a word. It felt like we were separate, in a bubble isolated from all the people and noise around us.

"Yes..." she said simply and that one word fused something inside me.

My eyes searched hers but they were closed to me now. We stood facing each other for what seemed like a century in this place that separated us and yet placed us together, like on an island where she and I were the only occupants.

"Cristina? Cristina?" Elena's voice broke the uncomfortable silence and brought me back to the reality of the night.

The spell was broken. I mustn't scare her away I told myself. Not now, not yet. I mustn't scare her away. That sentence kept going over and over again in my head.

"I'm sorry, Francesca. I was only nine when they died and I was ill for a long time afterward. My memories are vague at best. I always like to know people who knew them, but my enthusiasm sometimes gets the better of me. See you tomorrow?"

I looked at her, presenting a calmness I did not feel. She smiled and nodded.

"Tomorrow," she stated simply.

†

I tossed and turned all night. She knew them. She had acknowledged knowing them. She could clear up so many of my questions. I knew that. I felt I was right. She was the one who would be able to help me put it all together. My night was filled with thoughts and images of Francesca. I went over every word that was spoken with her and then gradually my mind tortured me and seduced me with the look of her. It was like an old film reel, black-and-white and silent. But, every aspect of her, every move was captured and enhanced perfectly.

I had to be patient; I had to move slowly. These phrases I repeated over and over again like a mantra within my brain. I had to be in control of the situation. I mustn't let my emotions rule my life as my parents had. They paid for their mistakes with their lives. This last thought disturbed me. Why did I think that? A haze seeped slowly into my mind, almost like a veil. I suddenly saw everything so clearly; too clearly. Clarity, what was it anyway but perception according to the individual.

People saw only what they wanted to see. My parents were led by their passions and sometimes their children got in the way. When that happened María and I usually got left behind. And the same old

21

resentments took hold again. Feelings of loss took hold so strongly within me that my breath became harder to reach my lungs. Control…I needed control.

Francesca had been the person I wanted to meet at that party. She had been the reason I went. I must also confess that I felt guilty. Perhaps that is why a part of me began to feel that thin thread of anxiety grow within. Why? I didn't know why. Yes I did, I knew exactly why. I had liked her. Why should that bother me?

Many times I thought of picking up the telephone and telling my grandmother I was coming home. But, deep inside I knew I would never do that. I wanted to know why the death of my parents had always been a subject that we never discussed.

The need to find out what had happened to them had become an obsession. What was it that people said? Obsession was the door that opened and led to madness…

The same litany repeated itself in my brain: I had lost María. I had lost María. Sometimes I could still remember her little hand in mine and how it felt. Her sweetness when entering my life filled me with that air that my lungs were never quite filled with. Perhaps that's what really prompted me to try to find out what had happened. I needed to make some type of sense of the loss. I craved a clean, clear breath…I had always craved that. There had to be a reason. It could not have been a simple accident. If so, why the mystery? Why not just tell me?

I had looked through newspaper clippings and articles written about the accident and all the horrid gossip that had followed. The speculations and the innuendos had been horrible, from my father's flirtatious nature to my mother's excesses of jet-setting parties.

I had dug through so many documents and newspapers from and about my parents. All I had was a name. That name was Annais D'Autremont. I had found it in my father's papers. Her name had also been entered in my mother's most desirable guests dinner list, which had been my mother's bible. Her name had appeared everywhere. She was also in the funeral attendance list. I had asked Grandmother about her once and all I heard from the other side of the phone was silence. She said she did not know her. But, I knew it was a lie.

Annais D'Autremont was someone who would be able to tell me more. I knew she was involved somehow. I could feel it. She would clear up some questions, I felt sure of it. Or at least be able to tell me more than what I knew or had guessed.

Why did I have to like her? Perhaps, it was just a coincidence with her name being all over. Perhaps I wanted answers so badly that I saw shadows where there were none.

And in that night a part of me awakened and in that fog I remembered words, a thought I had read somewhere in one of those melancholy afternoons of mine back in Spain. It was a quiet place on a large window seat in my grandfather's library. I would sit there on quiet, rainy afternoons and read. I liked it there, in that place of books, surrounded by something warm and familiar lightly tapping, wanting entrance…and the words from one of those old books came back to me.

> *Your eyes are closed to me now*
> *just as my heart is closed to you.*
> *A veil separates us…clear and copious like that fog that can be seen and not touched.*
> *And still I stare into it…*
> *Yearning…*
> *not quite knowing for what*
> *…but perhaps just for a shadow of you.*

In this memory I closed my eyes and finally slept.

Chapter Three

I had only slept a few hours that night. Nevertheless, I was showered and dressed for my luncheon with Francesca two hours early. I sat like a dressed-up mannequin on the sofa and waited.

So many questions went through my head as I waited; the two hours seemed to disappear until I was brought back to reality by the ringing of the telephone.

As soon as I heard her voice I knew instantly that it was Francesca. She offered to pick me up instead of meeting at the restaurant since it was sometimes hard to get a cab at the lunch hour. I accepted the lift and thanked her. She would be passing by to pick me up in about thirty minutes. I hung up the receiver and waited with anticipation.

That day when I first saw her in the light of day Francesca became a part of it, a part of me. She walked into my life that day and never left it again.

We went to Le Cirque for lunch. The setting had been orchestrated to impress. Francesca ordered for us. The waiter knew her by name. She was apparently a frequent customer. She asked to surprise me, and surprise me she did. And, yes, I was impressed by her choices. I guess it wasn't so much the choices but the combinations. Francesca was a woman of the world and was familiar with the trappings of wealth. It showed with her choices of foods and wines. Everything about her had an air of sensuality and allure that surprises me still.

Lunch was wonderful. I found myself just enjoying her company. I can admit, now, that I chose not to ask any questions that day because I just wanted to be with her. I didn't want my need to know answers to my questions to in any way break this elation I felt when I was with her.

"Why did you tell me your name was Francesca?" I asked her expectantly.

"Because it is..." she replied with a smile and said nothing else.

Her manner and her smile felt familiar, almost like a part of me. Neither of us referred to the past. We talked for hours about her travels and experiences, deciding to shop another day since we had stayed so long over lunch.

She would be away for a week and we agreed to meet on her return. I remember feeling incredible disappointment that she was leaving and a shadow of sadness seemed to take hold of me. It must have shown because her hand went over mine.

"I'll be back before you know it," she said gently to me.

I was looking at her hand on mine and then my eyes went to her face. There was always an aura of familiarity with Francesca. In that moment our eyes said more than any words could have. I looked down at our hands again in confusion.

"Would you like to come with me?" she asked quite suddenly.

"With you?" I repeated incredulously as I looked up.

"Why not? You would like St. Maarten. I'm building a house there and I must go and check its progress." She squeezed my hand as she smiled.

I was caught off guard, but the excitement must have shown on my face.

"Come on, come with me. You'll love the beach and the sun. It's so cold here now." It only took a minute for me to accept.

"Yes, I would love to come. Thank you, Francesca," I answered exuberantly.

She gave me the most beautiful smile I had ever seen. A few days later we were on a plane for St. Maarten.

Chapter Four

After the cold that had begun to be felt in New York, I remember how great the wave of heat felt as we got off the airplane in St. Maarten. We had flown in on a private plane and were met by a car at the tarmac of the airport. All details of the trip, including entrance details, had been seen to and Francesca noticed the question in my eyes as she returned my smile.

"One of the perks of money," she responded to my unspoken question as she entered the car.

I got in behind her and the chauffeur closed the door as I sat in the seat next to her. I stared out the window at the lusciousness of the flora all around us. As I opened the window next to me I was taken by the warmth of the air filled with the fragrances of wildflowers, combining with the smell of the ocean. I closed my eyes and sat back.

"You like…" she said with a giggle.

"Oh yes…"

It was a different world—a world with warm breezes and the rustling sounds of the tall coconut trees; a world filled with the blueness of an ocean never far away. It was a world of flowers; and was far away from all I had ever known.

The limousine took us to a villa on one of the resorts in St. Maarten. We were right on the beach and as I opened a window I felt the ocean breeze caress me. It felt so soothing to hear the rushing of the waves. At that moment I experienced a sense of freedom I had never quite been able to reach. Defenses that had been built over the years began to weaken; at that moment I began to feel a vulnerability that, although exhilarating, opened a door to a secret garden that my eyes were now willing to see. I took that first step without a thought.

I remember feeling so peaceful and quiet inside. Francesca came up behind me and put her hands on my shoulders. I looked back at her and smiled.

"Happy, Tina?" she asked.

My demeanor suddenly changed. The calmness that had filled me was gone, like a candle burning brightly and suddenly extinguished with the harshness of cold air. I felt angry, filled with a rage that shook my whole body and the coldness of so many winters alone covered my heart with a shell of impenetrable steel.

"Don't call me that," I said rather harshly.

I looked out to the ocean again, now with an invisible wall between us. She removed her hands from my shoulders as if my skin had burned her. I knew she was still quite close. I could hear her breathing. I could feel the warmth of her. I looked up and our eyes met in the reflection of the picture window in front of us. She was looking at me, questioning.

"Why?" she asked softly.

"I don't like it...I just don't like it." I wrapped my arms around myself in a protective gesture. I felt a shiver go through me. I felt cold and the same feeling of fog again seemed to be hovering, waiting for me, beckoning.

My anger disappeared as quickly as it had appeared and suddenly I was filled with fear. I looked in her direction, and not knowing why, my eyes filled with unshed tears.

She hesitated for only a moment, then turned me around and quickly took me into her arms. At first I tried pulling away, then just as quickly my arms wrapped around her. It was at that moment that the scent of her filled my senses and a part of me long forgotten surrendered to the warmth and softness of her. After a few minutes of bliss she held me at arm's length and spoke to me gently and with such sweetness that I would have done anything to be with her.

"It's so beautiful here, Cristina, why don't we go for a drive? Then we can go into the water when the sun is not that strong, hmmm?" She looked into my eyes in such a way that left me breathless.

I looked into her eyes and it was reassurance that I remember feeling.

"Okay," I replied all the anxiety forgotten, or so it must have appeared to her. How I wish it had; oh God how I wish it had.

Coming to St. Maarten with Francesca had been a crazy thing to do. I recalled thinking at the moment she asked that I had just met her. I was not only acting out of character but being driven by something that, in some ways, I had no control over and did not or chose not to understand. I had always been a quiet child and generally a cautious one. From the moment I had met Francesca, though, I realized all my decisions had been hasty and not thought out. I was taking chances I usually never took and coming with a total stranger to an unfamiliar place that was removed from all I knew was completely insane.

At that moment I looked up and my eyes followed her. She walked over to a small table near the door and took some keys from its drawer. She turned to me and put her hand out. I took it without the merest hesitation and we went for a drive.

St. Maarten was paradise I remember thinking as she drove. The island was divided into two parts— one was Dutch and the other was French. We were staying on the French part of the island. It only took a few hours to go around the whole island. At every turn there was ocean and sky. It was a world filled with sun, water, and a sweetness I had never known. A world filled with a wild landscape and flowers of vibrant colors. In those hours a distance had begun to grow. In those hours I distanced myself from the only world I had ever known. In those hours, we were driving away from something rather than to something. Like the Arcadian golden days...how we wish they would last forever, and, of course, they never do.

I had begun to relax again. After driving around most of the island we decided to do some shopping. I knew she came here often but we played tourists for the day for my benefit. We walked, going in and out of local shops. We laughed and simply delighted in the day.

It was around three in the afternoon when we headed back to the villa. I put on the bathing suit we had bought in town that Francesca liked and went out to meet her. She was already on the beach waiting.

She was sitting in a lounge chair wearing a big-brimmed hat, drinking some icy pink drink and wearing her sunglasses, elegant and ladylike. I ran past her and knocked her hat off. I was laughing with such abandonment and I knew that she was running after me, but I got to the water first.

I remember the joy of it. The splashing of the water, its coolness on my skin, and an abandonment of thought, it was so freeing that it made me giddy with joy. Eventually she caught me. We were splashing water at each other and she playfully pushed me under the water. She held me down and I was filled with panic. When I came up I gasped for air, frantically trying to fill my lungs with that which I had always been a constant to me—breath, I needed to breathe.

Francesca was immediately by me and embraced me. She was so tender. She pushed my hair away from my face and spoke gently to me. "I'm sorry if I frightened you, *mon petite cher*."

I clung to her. Still holding me she kissed my cheek and brushed my lips with hers.

I pulled back from her and swam away. She did not move until I turned and waved for her to follow, at which time she dove into the water and came after me.

We stayed in the water for an hour or so, splashing each other and playing like children for the remainder of the afternoon. Francesca reminded me of the carefree feelings of childhood, of their sweetness and the intoxicating allure of a sun-filled afternoon where no thought was required at all. She beckoned and like the Pied Piper, I followed her. After a while she asked if I was hungry. I was famished, I told her, so we swam back to shore to shower so we could go out to dinner.

†

We spent the next few days mostly meeting with her architect and inspecting the site where her house was being built. In the evenings, we would go out to dinner and finish up in some disco for the night.

I had begun to sleep badly again; the nightmares had started again and one night I remember dreaming that I was in a car and it was going very fast. I looked at who was driving and saw my father. He and Mother were arguing. I heard Mother scream and I saw us falling off a cliff. I sat up in bed screaming in terror.

Francesca rushed into the room and took me in her arms. I clung to her in the darkness for a life that I so desperately feared yet so desperately wanted.

"I went off the cliff with them... Oh god, they were fighting and the car went off the cliff." I said as I clung to her while sobbing into her shoulder. She tightened her embrace. I remember she held me so tightly to her that I could hardly breathe. Then I felt surrounded by the softness of her. She was gentle, her touch was so gentle...

"It's all right," she whispered into my ear.

"I don't want to be afraid anymore, Francesca. I don't want to be afraid," I confessed to her. "Hold me, please, just hold me," I pleaded as I cried.

"I won't let go," she said, reassuring me. I fell asleep in her arms that night.

Chapter Five

The days in St. Maarten that followed were uneventful, filled with sun and the sweetness of the mundane. We shopped in the morning and swam in the afternoons. Ever since the night she comforted me something had changed between us. There was a closeness that felt familiar and I was lulled with a sense of peace and contentment I had not felt in years. I wanted that sweetness to last forever. And the words of long ago rang through and came back to me again...

And in one instant,
I am filled with a sweetness of a summer's day,
The buzzing of the bees in a sea of green and the caress of the breeze

†

One day, Francesca asked if I would like to take a boat to a neighboring island with her. The island of St. Barths was legendary in the area for its wild beauty, surrounded by endless beaches and the beauty of an ocean from cliffs that took your breath away.

She hired a catamaran to take us over. We sat in the front part of the boat and as it rose with the waves we flew up what seemed like ten to fifteen feet and came quickly crashing down before another wave brought us up again. It was the most exciting thing I had ever done. I caught my breath before we were hit with yet another ascent up to the sky. Everything with Francesca was like that.

It took about two hours before we got to the island. Francesca hired a car to show us around. After some sightseeing of the older part of the island, we went to a restaurant that was right on the beach to have lunch, dining on crab bisque with white wine. Everything around us at the restaurant was wild and overgrown: ceiling fans of bamboo and bungalow-style, completely open, the sound of seabirds filled the air, overgrown greenery and the floral scents seeped into your system. I felt lazy and sleepy after the bisque and wine were finished. All that could be seen was ocean; all that could be heard was the sound of the rushing waves. This was another world, wild, beautiful, and filled with Francesca.

After we finished lunch we walked on the beach for a long time. Walking aimlessly, holding hands at times like two little girls when they are best friends and filled with the innocence of just being in the moment. We picked shells and no words were needed. There was a oneness with her in those moments that tied me to her; I never had a chance. Not that I wanted one.

Eventually, we sat down and just stared at the water. The rushing sound of the waves were soothing, so soothing. I laid back and closed my eyes. I felt her lift my head and put her jacket under it. My eyes were heavy. I was filled with a peacefulness I had once felt long ago and I took comfort in. And for the first time in a long time I slept peacefully.

We were in a bubble. Nothing and no one else existed. I felt at peace for the first time in a long time. All I could hear was the rushing sound of the sea and all I could feel was the breeze caressing my body. I was breathing in her perfume and her hair was brushing my face. My eyes closed and her lips lightly kissed mine. I smiled and fell asleep.

> *like being in a cloud, weightless...*
> *Held in a warmth felt long ago and long forgotten*
> *Surrounded by a perfume that filled all of me, it was familiar*
> *Like a lost wonderer my eyes were slowly opened and in the fog*
> *The vision was less shadow*

I remember her waking me. It was getting dark. I saw her smiling face over me. I stretched and smiled back.

"Welcome back, Sleeping Beauty," she said tenderly as her face came closer to mine. Her mouth softly kissed mine, her tongue tracing my lips lightly. I felt something alien stirring inside me; and at that moment it awakened. Kissing Francesca was losing myself to her. And I realized quite suddenly that I welcomed it.

I got up on my elbows and broke contact with her. Abruptly, the situation I found myself in hit home. A part of me wanted to escape and another wanted to surrender. She caressed my face with her hand slowly and then leisurely let it travel down my body. I felt her fingers lightly move over my breast, down my abdomen, then back up and down my thigh. I was frozen in her spell. I neither encouraged nor discouraged her. I could not breathe and for the first time I could remember I did not need to.

She never stopped looking at me as she did this. I just lay there and did nothing, basking in all the emotions awakened within me. When I was about to say something, she got up quickly and lightheartedly said, "Let's go, we'll miss the boat back," then started running down the beach.

I stared for but a second then I got up quickly and ran after her. We laughed as we both ran down the beach.

Back in St. Maarten the days were filled with the aura of sensuality, suntan lotion, and the sultry sea air. I had put the incident on the beach out of my mind or wanted to. I did not want to see. I did not want to feel what I was feeling. It was easier to just ignore it. And, as I had done many times before in my life, that is exactly what I did. I just put it away in a box to look at another day.

The last afternoon that we spent on the beach before our return to New York I started to ask her some questions. This borrowed time was coming to an end and I had to start thinking about what I had come for. At least, that's what I told myself. We were both lying on lounge chairs facing the water. It was easier that way. I had begun to realize that when I looked at her I would lose myself in her, lose myself in a wave of feelings that I would not be able to outswim. Almost at that instance the wave overtook me.

"Francesca, can you tell me about my parents?" It was a simple enough question as the words left my lips.

She showed no sign of discomfort. Without skipping a breath, she spoke. "What would you like to know?" She took a sip of her drink, never taking her eyes away from the water.

"All that you know," I said, looking directly at her now. I didn't want to play this cat and mouse game anymore. There was an urgency that had begun to grow inside me, an urgency that I now know the meaning of.

"That's a lot." She still did not look at me. Silence was her answer. I sat quietly waiting.

She got up suddenly. "Come on," she said, holding her hand out to me. "I've had a cabana put up down the beach so we could sunbathe before we go."

I just looked at her, not answering.

"We both have strap marks from the bathing suits. Come on, we'll talk there." I took her hand and we walked down the beach in silence.

Upon reaching the cabana she removed her top and turned to me so I could follow. I stood there not moving, barely breathing; just looking at her.

"Turn around and I'll unhook the back of your suit," she said with an air of such sensuality that I felt an overpowering, searing heat in my eyes that threatened to overwhelm me.

I turned around slowly and without objection. She unhooked my bikini top and let it fall to the floor. I turned around to face her, expectant. She smiled and lay down on a towel. I lay down next to her.

"The sun tingles," she said jokingly.

"Yes," I answered, laughing nervously.

"Have you ever sunbathed?"

"No."

"Here, put some lotion on my back, will you?" She turned her back to me after handing me a bottle of lotion.

I took the bottle from her and started rubbing the suntan lotion on her. Francesca's skin was bronzed and warm like the day itself. I put more lotion in my hand. I remember thinking that it smelled of coconut and slowly I caressed her back with it; to the point where I became lost in the warm feel of her skin.

She put her hair up as she turned slowly to look at me and lay down on her back. I knew she expected me to rub lotion on her chest, over her breasts and all I could do was stare at them. I sat motionless, not knowing what to do now, feeling quite juvenile holding a suntan lotion bottle and looking like a scared rabbit.

She took the bottle from my hand and gently said, "I'll put the rest on." She spread the lotion all over herself, not once looking at me. I lay back on my towel, relieved.

"Turn around and I'll rub some on you," she said.

I just stared, unsure, nervous, and it showed.

"Oh, come on, Cristina, don't be silly. You're going to get sunburned," she insisted.

Feeling rather foolish I turned my back to her. She rubbed her hands with the lotion and when she started to rub my back it felt warm. She rubbed the lotion in slowly, taking her time; I was so relaxed that I was lulled into a sense of security that, in retrospect, had never been there.

When she finished with my back, she asked me to turn around. Like her, I put my hair up and lay back on the towel. I reached out for the bottle but she did not hand it over; she stared at me and at that moment I saw the smokiness in her eyes before she looked away.

"I'm not embarrassed like you." She poured some lotion in her hands and began to rub them together.

I found out much later how truly close to oblivion I had come that day. I was like that moth again and the fire beckoned. And blindly I wanted to burn.

Her hands first came over my shoulders and down my arms. My eyes never left her face. Her hands felt warm as she stroked my skin over and over. And the fog enveloped me again…

> *The warmth of her touch was hypnotic and I was lost*
>> *Lost in the colors, in the rhythm, in the beauty of her and for one instant I thought the brightness…*
>> *She was the Sun*
>> *the sun whose kisses on my skin could burn…*
>> *and the lulling sound of the buzzing bees was hypnotic*

The way she was applying the lotion felt more like gentle caresses on my body. Her eyes… her eyes never looked away for a moment. It was then that my eyes sought and were imprisoned by hers. She started rubbing lotion on my sides and over my breasts. As she stroked them I began to feel my body pulsate. My eyes closed and as my mouth opened to gasp for air a groan escaped my lips. One hand stroked my breast while the other went over my abdomen. My breathing became hard and my body reacted. This was the birth of my desire for her. I didn't care. I wasn't thinking. I didn't want to. She did not force me to want her.

She poured more lotion into her hands and rubbed them together yet again to heat up the oil. My eyes closed then opened slightly as I saw her hands come over my breasts once more and when her lips came to meet mine, I welcomed them.

My mouth opened, welcoming her, returning her kiss. It was like a fire that spread quickly. I welcomed her tongue as it took mine and I felt my body move up to make contact with hers. Her mouth traveled down my neck and I could feel a hunger growing inside me that threatened to devour me. Her mouth traveled lower, and as it took possession of the erect and hardened nipple on my breast, a moan of raw desire escaped my mouth.

We then heard a surprised intake of breath that was like thunder to my ears. A young man, an attendant from the villa, had come upon us and stood staring in shock. I pulled away quickly, attempting to cover myself. Francesca was furious and started yelling in French at him. I cringed away, covering my nakedness with the towel.

I could have stopped her at any time; I knew that. But I chose not to for reasons of my own that I gave myself. Lies, all the reasons I gave myself were lies. I got up and walked out of the cabana. I kept telling myself that I would do anything, anything to find out what I wanted to know. I told myself that but I confess now that I could not help it. I never had been able to. I walked back to the villa in silence and in confusion.

Francesca followed after a while. I heard her moving about but she did not try to speak to me. Perhaps she too had needed the distance, I never knew.

I went to my bedroom, took a shower, pleaded a headache and went to bed early. We flew back to New York the next morning. We never discussed what had occurred. She acted as if nothing had happened and I followed suit.

Chapter Six

After arriving in New York I didn't hear from Francesca for the next few days. I think perhaps we both needed to process and understand what was happening between us. All I know is that I need the distance and perhaps she did too. I called my grandmother on the first day I got back but said nothing about my trip with Francesca. She had been feeling poorly and wanted me to come home. Something inside me told me over and over again that I should go. But, at the same time something kept me wanting to continue my search for the truth. I could hear the sadness in Grandmama's voice as she asked me to come home but my heart was closed to her pleas.

I got together with Elena for lunch that week. She told me all the news that my grandmother always omitted when talking to me about home, including the news that the royals had invited Grandmama to join them on a summer cruise to the island of Antigua. Grandmama had always viewed her position and her money with little importance. All that mattered to her was family and honor. My mother had given my grandmother her share of disappointments and the family money had more than once glossed over inappropriate behavior, as Grandmama used to say. She had hoped that after my mother married things might change. She had kept hoping when I was born that the birth of her first child might change things too. Neither of her wishes was granted.

Elena was pleasant enough during lunch that week. It was Alfonso I had a problem with. He was always so touchy and had not only a roving eye but his hands tended to overstep their boundaries as well. Elena either did not see these things or chose not to. We all lived in a world of illusions and mirrors.

It had been a week since I had last seen or spoken to Francesca, so when she called I was taken by surprise. I don't know what I expected but when I heard her voice I flushed and my cheeks burned from the fire I felt on my skin.

She sounded cold and distant. This surprised me somehow. I don't think I heard a word she actually said. All I knew was that I was talking to Francesca. She suggested we meet for lunch. I agreed. I had been sidetracked but realized I needed to get back to my reason for being in New York. Francesca would give me the answers I needed. At least that was the reason I gave myself for agreeing to see her. How ridiculously juvenile that sounds now. Every part of me had hoped for that call just as every part of me was alive again after it came.

She said she would pick me up within half an hour and I agreed. In almost exactly thirty minutes, my doorbell rang. I opened it knowing full well that it was she. When I opened that door it was like a gust of warm breeze caressed all of me. The smile and air of confidence I showed in no way was what I felt.

"Francesca, how lovely to see you again. Come in, please," I said to her politely and stepped to the side.

She kissed me hello on the cheek and walked in without saying a word. As she kissed me the scent of her perfume filled all my senses. As she walked past me, I again felt that pull toward her that I argued with myself didn't exist. My eyes could not help but follow her as she came into the room. How could I not stare—she moved with a sensuality that was hard to overlook.

She was dressed in a tailored gray linen suit that seemed to fit her body like a glove, accented with a silver-gray fox wrap around her neck. She had matching gloves and shoes and her hair was up and tucked in the back. She was the perfect picture of elegance and, as my grandmother would say, good breeding. How could I not stare; she was beautiful.

I realized I had been staring and looked away in embarrassment. She was looking at me in a very peculiar manner as well, I remember thinking. I moved behind a chair and placed my hands on it for support. I began to feel very uncomfortable as she did not say a word and just stared back at me. At the exact moment I was about to say something, the phone rang.

"Excuse me, Francesca." Relieved, I walked over to the phone to answer it. As I picked up the phone I thought to myself that this was a game, which, at that moment, I realized I might not be able to handle. Why I thought of it as a chess game I don't know. I had told myself I would know how to move the pieces along with great finesse; how truly innocent all those thoughts were, I realize now. Something inside me began to want to run that day.

I should have listened to that voice inside me. But I was young. And, when you are young nothing seems impossible. I was filled with a courage I did not have. I was not worldly. As much as I had traveled the world with Grandmama it had always been in a protective bubble. Nothing had prepared me for what was happening inside me. I thought I was so prepared. I could not have been more wrong.

I could feel Francesca's eyes on me and the sensation it awoke in my body. There was something about her eyes that seemed to go right through me and touch something inside me that gave my heart an extra beat.

I was shocked back to reality by the voice on the telephone. "Cristina…"

"Grandmama, is that you?" I felt like a bucket of ice water had been dumped on me. I turned away from Francesca quickly.

I could almost visibly touch the apprehension in the room. Francesca was nervous. I could see her reflection in the mirror to the side of me. At that moment I knew she was the key. The key players were now on the game board I told myself. I was so ridiculously confident then. How I wish I had just left then. I am lying to myself again. I would, nor could, never have left then.

"Grandmama, I'm fine. No, I won't be coming back in the immediate future. I want to stay here for a while longer. I've made a new friend and we are going out to lunch now." I could see Francesca's discomfort growing as she began to fidget with the gloves she held in her hands.

"Yes. I'll call you soon. *Te quiero mucho Abuela*." And with those loving words, I hung up the receiver. I turned to Francesca with a big smile on my face. The chase was on. It had become a challenge and she saw right through me.

"That was my grandmother from Spain," I told her as I picked up my own gloves and purse. I looked up to meet her eyes with a smile that slowly faded.

She walked unhurriedly toward me, stopping a few inches away. Her eyes searched my face and then locked with mine.

I stared at her questioningly. Her face got closer and her lips brushed mine. This should not have surprised me after what had happened on the island, but it did.

I heard the intake of my breath as my mouth opened in surprise. Then suddenly I realized I had been waiting for this. I stood frozen in fear and anticipation. I could only hear the pounding of my heart like loud drums in my ears. My breath began to feel strained.

She pulled back slightly and looked into my eyes again. I could begin to hear my heart beat faster, could feel the rushing sound as my blood moved through my body. I was vibrating with anticipation. After a moment, her lips found mine but this time I felt them open, and I could feel their warmth on mine. I mustn't let this game go too far, I told myself. I thought I was in control. Suddenly I realized that I was being pulled into the fire like the moth and like the moth it would kill me. I was falling fast into a vacuum I hadn't the strength to fight against. And did I want to escape? A part of me welcomed the burning, the heat that her fire would bring.

At that moment I felt her hand on my back, pressing me to her, and as if in slow motion I saw and felt my body melt into hers willingly. I hadn't the power or the desire to stop her. Her other hand cupped my breast while her thumb stroked my nipple. My head began to spin and as my eyes closed a groan escaped my lips. My mouth opened and I gave in to the growing need inside me.

I returned her kiss with a passion I had never experienced before. I pulled her to me with such wanton desire that I know it surprised her. She pulled away from me, putting some space between us. There was an odd look in her eyes. It appeared that Francesca had questions too. She was fighting for control. And at that moment I could see she had not planned on feeling this. The pleasure had surprised her. The pleasure had surprised me. We stood inches away, looking at one another. No words were spoken and yet our eyes said volumes. It was then, at that moment, that I saw the crack. How naïve I was.

As the passion of the moment faded, the smokiness of embarrassment and confusion replaced the desire in my eyes. She recovered much faster. Francesca stared at me in surprise and then went on the defensive immediately.

"You've never kissed a woman before!" She didn't ask, she stated.

She began moving about nervously, like something wild trying to figure out its next move.

"I have been asking myself that question after what happened at the beach that day. Your eyes wanted me to touch you but the signals were all wrong," she said to me. "You're what? Twenty-six now? Tell me, have you ever been with a woman?" She was yelling now as she stopped pacing and stared at me.

It never occurred to me to question how she knew how old I was. I just stood there, saying nothing, looking confused and speechless. My eyes looked down and my answer was a whispered "No."

After a long silence she spoke again, her voice angry. "You're just a baby, aren't you?"

I looked up in a mixture of anger and confusion. She was now pacing again nervously as her fingers touched her face.

"I am not, I'm of legal age!" I stated indignantly. She stopped and stared at me as if I was something foreign.

"You're playing a game you know nothing about. Have you even been with a man?"

"Yes," I answered too quickly.

"Liar," she said softly and started walking toward me slowly. She stopped directly in front of me. "You are playing with fire and you're going to get burned. Why don't you go home?" Her voice was soft as her eyes lightly caressed my face.

I was totally unprepared for this. What made me think I could handle something like this, I remember thinking at the time. The anxiety inside me began to grow out of control. The pounding in my ears grew louder and my vision began to glass over. My breathing became heavy and erratic and I started feeling dizzy.

"Stop it," she said. I just couldn't catch my breath. I started gasping for air as my hands clawed at her in desperation.

"You're hyperventilating. Calm down and breathe slowly."

She helped me to sit down on a chair. I clung to her arm in terror.

I tried to relax but it was impossible. I tried the breathing techniques I had been taught but to no avail. I released my hold on her, reached inside my purse and pulled out my inhaler.

She stood in front of me, staring. Fear was suddenly visible in her eyes.

I pumped the mist into my mouth. I couldn't catch my breath and I started to truly panic. In slow motion I could see the inhaler dropping from my hand to the floor. She quickly picked it up. I reached for her in terror and fell to the floor on my knees.

"Stop! Let me help you!" she yelled as reached for me. She put the inhaler in my mouth and pumped it. "Try to calm down," she said gently.

Francesca helped me up onto the nearby sofa. She started to unbutton my jacket and loosen my clothing to facilitate my breathing. After a while my breathing started to regulate itself a little. She never left my side, not for one second. My head fell back to rest on the back of the sofa as I gasped for air. I closed my eyes and tried to concentrate on the simple task of drawing in air to fill my lungs. That was my focus, breathing in and out.

Whenever this happened it always left me feeling weak and tired. My eyes felt heavy and my breathing was still erratic. I had never been alone during an attack. Always, there was the fear that if I were I might one day not be able to survive it. This trip to New York had been a step toward my independence, but my independence was short-lived.

She stood up and I reached for her. I was suddenly filled with fear of being alone. "No! Don't leave me!" I pleaded and the added excitement started my asthma attack once more.

I held on hard to her, as if by hanging on harder I could somehow get a breath of air into my lungs. She pushed me down onto the sofa and again helped me with the inhaler.

"I'm not going anywhere, you little idiot." Her voice was stern. "Calm down before you kill yourself." She sat next to me on the sofa and her hand stroked my face gently. "You foolish girl, breathe slowly. Come on, try." She whispered softly into my ear, "Close your eyes. I know what to do. Relax, Tina, just relax." She continued to stroke my face as she spoke gently to me.

Her strokes on my face were methodical and gentle. The focus on the touch of my skin had always helped, for some reason, to regulate my breathing. It made the panic gradually dissipate.

Slowly my breathing started to become more regular and less strained. My limbs felt like lead and my eyes felt so heavy that I could hardly keep them open. My lungs hurt. I hurt all over from the strain of trying to breathe. I don't know how long we sat there before I heard her voice from a distance. "I'll help you to bed, Tina."

Suddenly, I was nine years old again.

"I'll help you to bed, Tina," Mother said.

"No, I want to go with you and Papa," I protested.

"Will you stay with her?"

"Mama!" I cried.

"Carlotta, this can wait she needs you!"

"I'm taking care of this now. This is not the first asthma attack she has ever had." Her answer sounded very callous.

"Mama!" I cried in fear.

"Cristina, stop it!" She pushed my hands away from her.

"Go, I'll put her to bed. I'll stay with her," another female voice said.

"I'll tell him on the way. Be here when I get back?" Mother asked as she was leaving.

I was in bed and a cool hand was gently stroking my face. Lips were kissing my forehead.

"I'll stay with you, little one. Don't be afraid. I won't leave you alone." I was wrapped in a soothing embrace.

I opened my eyes ever so slightly and said, "No me dejes." *Don't leave me.*

"No, me quedaré contigo hasta que no tengas miedo y te sientas mejor mi pequeña." *I will stay with you until you are no longer afraid and you are feeling better, my little one.*

"Quiero ir contigo." *I want to go with you... I said.*

Out of the shadows I saw the face that had comforted me that day.

Chapter Seven

The face that came from the shadows of time was Francesca's. The same face I was looking at now. I stared at her in silence. Her face had hardly changed, I thought. Her beauty had matured but it was obvious to me that it had been her. My hand reached out for her face and I touched her cheek lightly to see if she was real or just a memory. My eyes could not get enough of her. I wanted to reacquaint myself with every contour of every detail. She was so beautiful; she had always been so beautiful.

She looked into my eyes and said sadly, "You were calling for your mother."

I looked away. "Was I?" I asked softly. She remained silent. I wasn't sure whether I was ready to tell her or if I wanted to. I just wasn't sure what would happen if she knew I had remembered her.

She got up and walked toward the window and my eyes followed her every move. It had gotten dark I noticed suddenly. I started to take in my surroundings. I was in my bedroom, but I did not remember getting there or into bed. I tried to sit up. A moan escaped my lips as the pain around my stomach and back became apparent. It was always this way; the pain always lingered.

She turned quickly and walked back over to me. She sat on the side of the bed and pushed me back down gently. "Relax or you may have another attack."

My eyes filled with unshed tears as I whispered, "It hurts." The tears started to roll down my cheeks. Her hand gently brushed them away.

"I know it hurts. I'll rub your back and sides and slowly you'll start to feel better." Her gentleness only made the tears roll faster down my cheeks. Why was the only word that filled my mind. There were so many whys, so very many.

She removed the sheet covering me and by doing so revealed my nakedness to me. I looked up at her as she started to rub the sides of my ribcage. My eyes must have shown surprise as to what she was doing.

"The doctor showed me how," she gently answered my questioning eyes. "Don't talk; the strain will make you hurt more. Just relax and it will feel better."

She continued to massage my sides rhythmically. "I called my doctor. He came right away and gave you an adrenaline shot. Apparently your attack was rather severe, he said. He also left a prescription of prednisone for you to take for the next few days. That should help you feel better." Never did she make eye contact as she said all this to me.

I just listened as she continued to speak. I was mesmerized by the sound of her. Images of her kept crashing into each other in my mind. Francesca, she was Francesca…

"Dr. Cardoval is a friend. Luckily, I was able to catch him at home."

She continued to gently massage me and then quite suddenly she plunged right in. "Why are you here alone, Cristina?"

I turned my face to look at her and was met by the familiar eyes of a stranger. I said nothing. My eyes sought hers out for comfort. I was so tired. I just wanted to let go and drown in her softness.

Her hand then caressed my face and her lips brushed mine as she softly said, "I'll stay with you till you are better, little one." My eyes closed and I fell asleep.

> *And again the darkness cradled me*
> *An old friend...in its gentle arms I sought*
> *oblivion*
> *All I wanted was to rest and surrender;*
> *to drown in the security of its familiarity and*
> *its nightmare*

I woke from the fog a few times throughout the night and felt her close by in the darkness. The pain kept waking me as I turned in bed. I felt her hands gently comforting my aching body and in the morning I woke to the warmth of her. I could feel her breath on the back of my neck and her arms wrapped around me, holding me close to her. Holding me...

Oddly enough, it felt right. It was familiar, not new. I felt warm and leaned back into the softness of her body until it dawned on me that I was in bed, naked, in the embrace of a woman. My body suddenly tensed and almost immediately I felt her come awake. Her arms tightened around me.

"Are you all right?" The concern was apparent in her voice. I turned on my back to look at her.

"That's some question, taking this scene into account," I answered. A great big smile appeared on her face.

"Well, I can see you put up a great act," she answered. She leaned down and kissed me on the lips. Just as quickly she jumped out of bed.

"I'm starving," she said as she started dressing. She had been wearing a shift; I, however, had been quite naked. She turned to look at me.

"Well, what would you like for breakfast?" she asked humorously as her smile filled the room.

I shook my head. "No, I couldn't eat a thing."

"Well, perhaps just some tea." I nodded my head. "Would you like to get up or to stay in bed?" Her voice caressed me seductively with every word.

I stared at her nervously.

"Don't look so worried. The day I take you to bed it will be because you want to, not because I forced you," she said to me very seriously, not letting me for one moment gloss over what was obvious to her and what I did not want to admit.

"I can never love you," I told her suddenly, not even trying to dispute her words.

She stared very soberly into my eyes. "We'll see. I'll get the tea." She turned and walked out of the room, closing the door behind her.

She came back into the room about fifteen minutes later with a tray in her hands. Her eyes searched the room and found me sitting in front of my dressing table, combing out my hair. In her absence, I had put on a pink silk robe that had hung in my closet. It had been a Christmas present from Grandmama, and I confess I used it as a shield against her.

She put the tray down on a nearby table and walked over to stand behind me. She put her hands on my shoulders, knelt down and I could see the reflection of her face in the mirror next to mine.

"You really are exquisite," she said, looking at me. I stood up quickly and moved away from her. I needed to put some distance between us.

"I think you have gotten the wrong idea about me!" I said, staring at her with a confidence I knew I didn't have.

"What idea is that?" she asked as she looked around in boredom.

"I'm not like you. I don't like women!" I blurted out. She looked at me for a long time, searching my face for something.

"I see," was all she said. She turned away from me and started to pick up the rest of her things from around the room.

I was unsure of what to do. I had to stop her; I couldn't let her go.

"Francesca, I like you but not like that," I finally said as she opened the door of my bedroom. She turned around and I could tell she was angry.

She threw everything on the floor and started walking quickly toward me. I took a step back and she stopped suddenly about three feet away from me.

"Make up your mind, darling, because I'm losing my patience."

"Why must it only be your way?" I asked.

She thought for a moment and then she lashed out. "You knew the night on the veranda about me, you knew I liked you. When I've kissed you, you've kissed me back, and I know you enjoyed my touching you. If it hadn't been for the interruption in the cabana that day, well...who knows, wouldn't you agree? Have I forgotten anything here?" She had pointed out all the obvious truths.

I found myself unable to answer. I sat down on a chair nearby. A long silence stretched between us. I spoke but was unable to look her in the eyes.

"I did enjoy...all that you said is true. But I...I don't want..." I looked up at her standing before me and continued, opting for the truth. "I'm afraid." I was barely audible.

She turned her back to me and walked over to where she had thrown her clothes and started picking them up again. "Damn," she said in regret. She lowered her head as if considering what to do. Her head came up and she placed the clothes on top of the chair near the door.

She turned around and walked toward me very slowly. Her hand reached out to me and my hand went out to meet hers. I stood now in front of her. Her hand came up as if to caress my face but stopped before reaching it.

"I can't be just your friend. This will never work, I never meant for it to go this far. It's better if you just let me walk away."

No! I could hear in my head. No! Don't let her walk away! She was the closest I had ever come to finding out about the death of my parents, I couldn't let her leave! I turned my back to her and folded my arms in front of me.

I needed time. I needed Francesca, but how far would I go to keep her close? And of course, I also asked myself if I was just trying to find an excuse to absolve my guilt about this type of relationship. Deception, I was drowning in the deception of my own making.

I needed time. She had hesitated for a reason. That was the card I had to play. I turned and faced her.

"No, I don't want you to go. I need you to tell me that you'll give me time." I played my hand.

"NO!" she exclaimed.

"No?" I asked. I had lost.

She started putting on the rest of her clothes. I just stood there, watching her get ready to walk out. She finally put her shoes on, got up, walked toward the door, and out of my bedroom.

"Francesca!" I yelled going after her.

She was halfway to the front door and stopped with her back to me. "My name is Annais. Annais D'Autremont. If you ever call me Francesca again we will both understand what that means." She started walking to the front door and out of my life.

She had reached the door and as her hand touched the handle I said in desperation, "I'm afraid to be alone."

She lowered her head a little but she did not turn to me. She would never meet me halfway. "It's better this way," she said softly as she opened the door and started to walk out.

"Francesca!" I yelled out to her as I fell to my knees.

My hands covered my face as tears came forth. My cries became sobs and then I felt her arms around me, and I reached out and clung to her.

"Okay...okay don't cry anymore," she kept saying. Sobs shook my body. My tears were not for her, they were for me. I felt myself lifted into and turning out of control in an endless funnel.

"Okay, calm down. We don't want you to become ill again," she whispered softly to me.

I looked up to her not quite knowing what to expect.

"Don't look like that. I'm not going to make love to you now on this floor." She started stroking my hair. I was silent. "We have to get you well now and you need not be afraid, I'll not leave you alone." As she said this she helped me up from the floor.

I lost myself in the arguing, the words...
I lost all the arguments that were never truly real.

*I lost hold of what had kept me asleep for so
many years.*
I lost...

She held me to her and as I looked into her eyes I
saw there something that surprised me.

"From the first moment I saw you I wanted you.
Something inside me told me that knowing you would
change my life forever. For a moment that night, I
thought that I better just pass you by. Then you
walked out to the veranda and saw me. When I saw
you blush I knew. I knew that I had to make you mine
or I would die wanting you. When I found out who
you were...I should not have come, God forgive me, I
should have stayed away. I don't want to hurt you, I
just can't help myself...I want you so badly it hurts."
As she fell quiet, I found myself once again not
knowing how to respond to her.

She pulled me closer to her with one hand and
with the other she started wiping my tears away.
*"Mon, petit cher, je te necesite avec moi, tu ne me
necesite pas, mais je te necesite, pardonez
moi...pardonez moi."*

I looked at her in complete bewilderment. I could
only imagine what she was saying by the softness in
her voice. "I don't understand."

"I'll show you." As she said this the hand wiping
away my tears went around my neck and pulled me to
her.

Her lips were warm and inviting and just as
before my body seemed to catch fire. I did not try to

fight her, even for a second. This time my response came faster than before. I wanted to feel her body next to mine. My hands went up her back and I pressed myself closer to her. I wanted to lose myself in her.

I told myself that I was prepared to do anything to find out about my parents. But I know now, as I knew from the very beginning, I did not want to face the fact that I was also filled with desire for her.

Her touch filled me with a hunger I had never known. At that moment I was the one that wanted and I let my hunger lead the way.

The passion between us exploded and spread quickly throughout my body. All I wanted was to go on feeling. Francesca had been right: I had never been with a man or a woman. I had been allowed to have admirers. They had kissed me and fondled me, but I had never felt this fire, this hunger that knew no end.

Her mouth traveled to the side of my neck. I felt my back arching as she parted my robe and cupped my breast. Her mouth descended to my breast and covered my nipple. I inhaled at the pleasure, panting with desire as her mouth traveled over my breasts. I became giddy with the excitement and felt myself leave the world and float away in a cloud of pleasure.

Chapter Eight

Each breath I took resonated in my ears like
an avalanche
Lost in a sea of something foreign
Running toward an abyss
Endless in the wanting and...
Lost in its wake.

We lay in bed all day. The outside world simply did not exist; I did not want it to. I had never imagined feeling so much pleasure. And like a lost traveler in the desert she was like water to me. I was filled with such a thirst for her that I thought I would never be able to quench it. Francesca enveloped all of me and at that moment I wanted to only feel the perfection of the emotions she brought forth in me. I wanted this. Every road would have inevitably brought me to this.

I looked out the window and it was dark again. I had known her for less than five weeks. So much had happened in such a short time. She was so much a part of me now. It had been like a roller-coaster ride I had been on when I was very little. It had enticed and frightened me but what a thrill it had been. Each breath I took resonated in my ears like an avalanche of sounds and emotions.

I had never in my life felt such contentment as I felt lying in her arms at that moment. Could it last? Did I want it to? All I knew, and all that mattered, at that moment was being in the moment. I loved the feel of her and again I reached for her...

Later, as I lay in her arms, a voice inside me warned that I should never have come to New York. The past would catch up with me eventually and I would have to pay the price. But, that day I thought I was still mistress of my fate. How naive. I didn't know anything of the world, how could I know anything about me. I pressed myself to her and felt her embrace tighten as she kissed my forehead. At that moment that was all that mattered. I wanted Francesca—no I needed Francesca. And again the questions of a buried past taunted and haunted me. Her voice brought me back...

"We have to get some food into you," she mumbled softly.

"Not hungry."

"A Coke?" she asked jokingly.

"Nah."

"Let me take care of you," she said.

I felt my body tense. I sat up on the bed suddenly. "I don't need you to take care of me." My reply was harsher than I had meant it to be.

She was sitting next to me almost immediately. She tried touching my shoulder and I brushed her hand away.

"What's the matter with you?" she asked.

"There's nothing the matter with me. You were very clear about what you wanted. Now I'm telling you what I want and don't want." I lashed out.

She just stared at me in confusion, trying to take in the scene and figure out what was happening. I started to get up and her hand grabbed my arm.

"Why are you acting this way?" she demanded.

"Isn't this what you wanted, Francesca? You wanted to get me in bed. You wanted it your way. Well, we did it your way. What do you want now?" I blurted out in impatience.

"Don't tell me you didn't want to do this!" she exclaimed.

I said nothing.

I could see the anger rising in her face as she went on the attack.

"Dammit! Dammit, I knew this was going to be a tempestuous love affair," she yelled, getting out of bed. "Don't you insinuate that I forced you into this! You knew what you were doing!"

She was pacing and growing angrier by the minute. "I won't take responsibility for your guilt now, do you hear? I have never, never..." she ended her tirade very quietly and turned her back to me.

She turned toward me, faced me and very slowly started talking again. "I didn't intend to make love to you today. But, I also knew if you didn't accept the thought of it today you never would." She kept speaking as I just sat in the bed listening. "I just intended to kiss you. I didn't expect your reaction. I wasn't the one who initiated our lovemaking. You must see that?"

"Lovemaking?" I asked sarcastically.

She looked at me in bewilderment. "What do you think this was?"

"You wanted me; you don't love me, FRANCESCA!" I emphasized her name sarcastically, throwing her it back at her.

"Is that what is bothering you? You think that I'm just using you?" she asked incredulously.

I did not respond.

"I am not your mother!" she yelled.

"Shut up! Just shut up!" I yelled back, covering my ears so as not to hear anymore.

She took a step closer and very slowly started talking. "I have never felt such passion for anyone." She paused. "When I called you on the phone I had every intention of never seeing you again. But I couldn't stay away. I tried to...you must believe that." She came to sit next to me. "I found myself in love with you. I wanted to see you, but I didn't plan on this. You're so young," she spoke softly. As she continued to stare at me, her eyes became smoky with desire.

"I'm not that young, Francesca," I said with a touch of sarcasm.

"From the first moment I saw you at my party I fell in love with you. Before I knew who you were..."

After a little while she lay back down on the bed and opened her arms to me. My eyes scanned her beautiful body. How could I have forgotten her?

The memory of her came back to me as through a fog. Slowly, it came back to me and before I knew it, I was surrounded by it. I was in a bubble with her; the world did not exist. God how I wished for that, how I wished I could have just stayed with her.

I had seen her in a bathing suit once, when I was young, and I remember admiring her beauty. She was something distant and unreachable to me. Even then something inside me had recognized her.

And again the fog gave way and I remembered playing with my sister in the pool and Francesca was sitting close by, talking to my mother. She had hardly changed and again I shut the memories out.

Now as she lay back on my bed, I found my hands caressing her body. When they reached her breasts, I could see how excited she was. Her nipples were hard and her arms reached out to pull me to her. I could not only see but feel her desire for me.

I grabbed her hands and pinned them over her head as I lay on top of her. I was teasing her lips, barely brushing them with mine as my body rubbed against hers.

"I love you," she whispered and my mouth still kept teasing her. I could feel her body moving beneath mine, trying to get some release from my taunting.

"Please tell me you love me," she pleaded as tears rolled down her face.

"Now we do it my way," I said as my lips opened and I started kissing her in earnest.

†

Later that night she brought me food and fed me in bed. She was no longer in charge of this game. I had taken the queen and the game board had completely changed.

Walk with me, stroll with me through this garden.
Hold my hand and keep it close to your heart.
And the colors filled my senses but the fog had never been far behind me.

I was awakened the next morning by the ringing of the telephone next to my bed. I reached for the receiver and slowly reality began to seep in.

"Hello?" I mumbled into the phone, half-asleep.

My eyes immediately opened and I quickly sat up in bed.

"Grandmama!" I said in surprise and proceeded to wrap a sheet around me. "No, I was just asleep," I told her. "I'm fine, really. Yes, I haven't forgotten. I need to do this. We have talked this out already. I'm sorry, Grandmama. I don't want to hurt you but I can't just let it go. Yes, I promise. How is Tomás? I miss him too. I'll call soon. *Te quiero mucho. Adios."*
I replaced the receiver on its holder with my back to Francesca.

I could feel Francesca looking at me. "Who is Tomás?" she asked suddenly, completely surprising me.

"My cat," I replied.

I had not moved after hanging up the telephone. I just sat there looking straight ahead. She said nothing else.

"You knew my parents?" I spoke without moving, knowing what the answer would be.

"Yes," was all she said.

"You knew them very well." I insisted.

There was a long pause before she spoke this time.

"Yes," she finally answered, barely audible.

Still, neither of us moved. The room was filled with an ominous silence.

"I love you," she finally whispered. My eyes closed and I took in a deep breath then turned slowly to face her. The anger, that old monster inside me, found its way, there was no going back.

My eyes were not forgiving. I could see fear in her eyes as tears ran down her face. At that moment she was about to say something, and I did something rather strange that to this day I have not forgiven myself for. I placed my fingers over her lips. I did not want to hear the words. I needed time. I wanted more time with her. And at that moment I did not want nor did I deny my need of her.

"Not now...not today," I told her.

She threw herself into my arms and started crying in earnest.

My arms went around her and I stroked her hair as I held her close to me. I moved in with Francesca a few days later.

Chapter Nine

I had made up lie after lie each time I spoke to my grandmother as to why I was never home when she called. I kept the apartment, of course, and would pick up my messages twice a day. I had a cleaning service come in and clean once a week. The place had to be kept as if it were lived in. I had become an expert at fabrications. The web I was weaving took on a life of its own and it spread before I even realized it; I spun the loom and waited like a predator in the furthest rim. Odd that I thought that.

After a while I had put out of my mind completely why I had come to New York. I liked being with Francesca. I liked going to bed with her. She made me feel alive and I hadn't felt alive for so long. If I could keep my two worlds apart, I might actually be happy. Why did I think that? Why did I want the world at arm's length when it came to her?

What was happening to me? This lie of a life I was living was more real than anything else I had ever experienced. It was as if all that had ever happened in my life had occurred to prepare me for this. I would enjoy it for as long as it lasted. My emotions became stronger and harder to control every day. It was as if there were two people constantly fighting for dominance inside me.

†

When we had been living together for over three months, I found myself wanting to share so much with her. I could have been mistaken about her suspected involvement with the death of my parents. It wasn't entirely impossible. I wanted to believe that. Oh God, how I wanted to believe that. I wanted her; I wanted her so very much in my life that I built my life around her and for her.

We were careful not to talk about my parents and as if by silent signals we avoided not only conversation but also words. Because words can make you happy and words can end things and take all the air away from your lungs. We both moved carefully as if around eggshells. We tried so hard not to move too quickly. Our relationship was so fragile and we tried so hard. However, somehow no matter what, there were moments that we realized this peace would not last.

Socially, we both knew there was an invisible line that we must not cross. We both respected those boundaries. Our public outings were limited to certain clubs, places that were private and were not frequented by the people she knew and the few that might know me.

We never discussed doing this intentionally but we both understood when the other would hint that we should not go to this place, or that we should try another. I knew that Francesca had practically given up her social life by the messages she never returned.

When we were both seen in public we were politely friendly. People might very well comment that we were polite strangers that met by chance on several occasions. I would occasionally go out with Elena and Alfonso because I knew that my grandmother, as a matter of conversation with Elena's grandmother, asked about me and what I was doing. And her grandmother, like mine, had a tight hold on Elena.

One day, Francesca had gone out to some committee meeting and I had gone shopping. It had been a day like so many others. I liked living in the United States. I liked the variety of cultures, foods, and music. I bought a few CDs of different kinds of music and had found that I had begun to like some country musicians. I liked Patsy Cline, in particular, and bought an old album newly released on CD. I was listening to the music when Francesca arrived home.

"Oh God, what is that you're listening to?" She wrinkled her nose in playful mockery as she pulled off her gloves and looked through the mail that she had picked up on the way in.

"Patsy Cline," I replied with a smile. Some of my new taste in music really drove her crazy.

"I don't know how you can like that," she said, walking all around the packages I still had on the floor from my shopping odyssey.

"Oh, come on, Francesca, give it a chance," I joked with her.

She shook her head and laughed.

"You should get off your patrician pedestal and give it a shot. Let down your hair, as they say here in America." I laughed.

"Oh God, I can't believe an Alcalá saying that." Almost immediately she realized she had made a mistake.

I stood up in front of her. "Well, you should know!" I spit out.

She froze.

My eyes grew cold and feelings that I had tried to bury came to the surface. We were surrounded by the loud music and as it floated by we were as still as if we were in a picture frame. The song playing was of love and the pain that old memories bring. The words touched me so deeply that my memories broke the stillness.

> *Memories that do not seize invade and I...*
> *I reach for you and the image wavers*
> *And something inside me knows*
> *I will never touch you.*

Quite suddenly, in a small instant, I saw her and mother laughing together. Then my mother embraced her. They noticed me in the room and Francesca suddenly pulled away.

I quickly walked over to the CD player and turned off the music. I blinked the memory away.

Like an old picture show of slides, flipping images, slowing down, stuck in between images.

I started picking up packages and took them to the bedroom, leaving her standing in the living room. I threw the bags on the bed and went back to get the rest. I found her standing in the same place I had left her in.

"I thought you would return later so I accepted an invitation from Elena and Alfonso for dinner," I said as I picked up the rest of the packages.

"Tina, let me explain," she pleaded.

I turned quickly toward her. "Don't! We have an understanding!" I yelled furiously.

"Tina, please let me explain," she said again.

"Don't call me that! Don't ever call me that! EVER!! We have an understanding. Never forget it again!" I demanded.

I shook with anger. She had broken our agreement. She had made me see inside myself and I hated her for it. I leaned forward against the back of a chair and stared into space, trying to escape myself.

I felt her as she came to stand next to me. She tried touching me but I pushed her hand out of the way. My action made her take a step away from me. It had been worse than if I had slapped her. The phone started ringing and I walked over to answer it. There was a part of me that could always be cold and unfeeling. That is the person that had left Spain; that could leave a beloved grandmother, knowing that every step and every action cut into her. It was a part of me I had always denied. And so when I could take a step away from Francesca I did not even think twice about it. After all, how could I deny who I was?

"Elena, yes, I'm at Francesca's apartment, can you pick me up here?" I had my back to her now. Elena agreed to pick me up. "Okay Elena, I'll see you in an hour." I hung up the phone.

I looked toward Francesca but she looked away from me. She had her arms around herself protectively. A sob escaped her mouth as she raised her eyes to meet mine. Tears were running down her face. She opened her mouth to say something but did not. I walked over to her, my eyes softening. I had cut her and now was consoling her. And yes, I never made the connection that, at that very moment, I was more an Alcalá than even she or I knew.

"Why don't you come to dinner with us?" I asked her with a half-smile, as if all that had occurred had been a lover's quarrel. Her eyes searched mine and I touched her face lovingly.

"No," she said softly, looking down. She was afraid and so was I. I had to tread softly. It could all fall apart. I told myself that I was still in control of my relationship with her, of my feelings for her. I gave myself so many reasons.

"Okay, I'll cancel dinner with Elena and stay with you." She looked up immediately with tear-filled eyes. "We'll stay here, together," I said as I caressed her face. Her eyes asked for so much. And there was only so much that I could give her but I wanted to; God, I so wanted to, I so wanted to just give all to her.

She rushed into my arms and clung to me. "I don't want to lose you."

I put my arms around her and held her tightly to me. "I couldn't live without you. Don't you know that by now?" As I finished saying this I found her lips. All I wanted to do was feel. I didn't want to think anymore. I canceled my dinner plans with Elena.

†

Something had woken me in the middle of the night. I had been startled by noises. I got up and went to my window. There were two people fighting. I could hear them from my window. I opened the door that led from my room to the garden. The grass felt wet under my feet and it tickled. All I could see were my two little feet walking through a garden then I saw them quite suddenly. My father was kissing Francesca.

My eyes popped opened and sat up in bed, feeling disoriented. I looked next to me and saw her sleeping. She was so beautiful. She looked so innocent. If only she were. Oh God, how I wish she were!

I got up and reached for my robe at the foot of the bed. I sat down on a chair facing Francesca's sleeping body. I loved her. It suddenly became crystal clear to me that I had fallen in love with her.

What a joke life had played on me. The doctors had said that one day my memories might come back. I had wanted to remember so badly. At first it was just a feeling but lately the feelings were becoming real. Now my memories were destroying what I had left of my life. I had loved her even then. Not as now, but it had been love nevertheless. I loved her out of need even then.

No more! I shut my eyes. *I don't want to remember any more.* I wanted to forget what I already knew. I was happy. Was it so wrong to want to be happy?

I remembered bits and pieces. I suspected the rest. The memories would come a piece at a time and I never knew when. Usually they were triggered by something she said or something we did. I was caught in a trap of my own making. I had always thought of myself as the spider in the web, not the fly; is that what I was, or was I the fly instead? Confusion reigned in my mind and the bits and pieces never quite added up.

I had started to daydream a lot. I would seem to drift away and usually she would touch my arm lightly and I would come back to the present. My eyes would search hers and she would look incredibly sad. It was at these moments that I loved her best, when her eyes would hold me with such gentleness that all I wanted was to be with her forever.

"I wish we could just make the rest of the world disappear for us," she said one day. I remember smiling…the past; why was I always drifting to the past.

Something awakened her. She reached for me and found only emptiness. She sat up in bed and her eyes found me sitting in a chair against the wall facing her.

"Tina?" she called out.

"Yes," I answered softly. The silence grew between us. "I love you, Francesca," I said to her in the dark.

She was motionless.

I walked slowly to her.

She was still; afraid that if she moved the moment would disappear. Did she know? Did she know even then?

I let my robe fall to the floor and allowed my naked body to make contact with hers. The moment my skin met hers a fire took over all my reason. And as had happened many times before I surrendered to my hunger to possess her. She moved beneath me and my body responded. My mouth sought hers and it fused to her with a hunger to devour. I wanted her. I needed her. I had wanted her my whole life. And nothing would take her from me, not even the past. This was the first night I truly made love to her. No agenda, no thought, I loved her with all of me.

†

Two weeks later I received word that my grandmother had had a heart attack and I was to come home at once. That day Francesca found me sitting in the dark when she got home. My life was catching up with me. I could feel it. The dark clouds were rolling in and there was nothing I could do to stop them. Nothing could hold back the storm now.

Francesca and I agreed that I should go alone and then arrange things for her to follow later. She had agreed to my leaving without her after much debate. I needed the comfort of her and yet she was the last person I wanted to be with me at this time. This made no sense just as my life made no sense. How could I tell her that it was because I loved her that I didn't want her to come? I left for Spain that same night.

I arrived in Spain nine hours later exhausted and numb. It was all hazy again like so many other times. I could feel the pain invading my very being. Although I wanted to detach from all these emotions that came upon me like a flood I knew I could not, so I moved forward to the inevitable.

Within two hours of my arrival I was running into my grandmother's house. I ran straight up to her room. She died thirty minutes later. It was finished. I remember walking out of her room without saying a word. I went inside the library and locked the door. I sat in that nook where I had so many times in the past. I picked up that old book that had always been such a favorite, still lying there as if waiting for my return. And the pages beckoned and the words followed.

And in the past she stood next to me…

"¿Qué lees mi niña?" How lovingly she asked what her beloved child was reading.

"Poesías abuela, poesías de una escritora Americana." I pointed to the cover of the book. It was a poetry book by an American poet.

She smiled indulgently as she always had. There was always so much love in those eyes for me. Grandmama had always loved me and never failed to tell me.

"Me alegro mi Niña. ¿Cómo se llama esta poetisa?" S. Anne Gardner es la poetisa, me gusta mucho. Encontrée el libro con los libros de el abuelo." Innocently I had taken one of the books that my grandfather had loved reading.

She turned pale suddenly and sat next to me. Her hand shook a little as she caressed my face and her eyes again looked into mine with so much sadness.

"Mi poesía favorita se llama La Neblina. *¿Quieres que te la lea abuela?" My words had been lost to her as I asked if she wanted me to read to her. She merely kept staring and caressing my face.*

And the past faded into the present again…

It all seemed so unreal. I was wrapped in a haze I could not breathe in. And yet I knew that if I were to venture out of it, it would kill me. My grandmother was dead. And with her went the last living person who knew the real truth.

After a few hours I walked up the stairs to where her body rested. I passed by weeping servants. I reached the door to her bedroom and turned the doorknob. Walking in I slowly went to the foot of her bed. Her body lay there motionless. I stayed in the room alone with her until they came to take her body away. I spoke to no one.

Chapter Ten

A week later, dressed in mourning clothes, I sat in front of her lawyer, Licenciado Marcelo Bustamante. He had arranged this meeting so that her Last Will and Testament might be read. She had been buried quietly with no viewing. There had been a private mass and then she had been placed in the family mausoleum next to my mother.

I sat in silence as they read how she wanted her property distributed. She had left some things to close friends and people who had served her throughout the years, but the bulk of her estate was left solely to me. I had not known until that moment how truly wealthy my family had been. I was now a very wealthy woman. After signing all the required papers the attorney handed me an envelope.

"Your grandmother asked that you be given this envelope upon her death." I took the envelope from him. "I presume you want the present arrangements to remain in place at the hospitals?"

I looked at him in surprise, but nodded my agreement in silence. I can't even say that I was in shock because that would actually require some type of emotion that I just didn't feel. What I remember the most about that meeting was my sense of detachment. I felt nothing. There was no emotion inside me. She had never said anything to me about her plans, and I remember that at that moment I hated her for not having given me a choice. I had never ever been given a choice. Not ever, not by anyone. I took the envelope and nodded.

"Gracias," I said, then got up and walked out of his office.

I don't know how long I walked. I just walked. I needed to keep moving. If I stopped the pain would catch up with me. If I stopped I might have to see what I was running away from. There were so many emotions all crashing within me at the same time. And her eyes would always come back to me. She had always been there to love and protect me and I had left her. I had left her alone and denied her that time she had left without me.

I was torn between anger and guilt. I should have been with her. Every time I spoke with her she was asking me to come home. She must have known she was dying. She needed me and I had not come. She had loved me, nursed me, scolded me, consoled me, and taught me right from wrong and never for one moment complained. She had also deceived me. I was all she had in this world and knowing she was ill, I had left her. She should have told me. God, she should have told me. All these thoughts kept crashing into one another and the weight of them were tearing down something that I could not hang on to.

†

After walking about for hours I arrived home to be met with a message from Francesca. She was in Spain and wanted to see me. She was staying at the Ritz-Carlton in Madrid. I went into the library without saying a word after Jaime, the major-domo, had given me the message. I had to think but my mind was so tired of thinking that it hurt.

I sat behind the desk and dialed the number that Jaime had handed me. I hung up the phone before the second ring. I wanted to hear her voice but a part of me ended the call. I couldn't do this. I was afraid. I wanted to run to her for comfort but I was afraid. Why was I so afraid? In truth all I truly remembered within me was fear.

I had not contacted her since my arrival. I don't know what she could be thinking or if she would stay. All I knew was that I couldn't do this anymore. My past had haunted me my whole life and now it was going to kill me. This truth became very clear to me. The choice was clear; if I chose Francesca it would probably kill me. I might still survive this if I never saw her again. Why? Why had life conspired against me? I wasn't sure exactly why I thought this; all I knew was that the only thing inside me cried for her. I need the warmth of her, her arms around me, her lips on my skin. Even the sound of her my body and soul craved.

I went upstairs to my room, removed my clothes and went to bed. I wanted to close my eyes and never wake up again. When I laid my head down on my pillow the tears just came. For a week I had not been able to cry and now I was drowning in them. I cried for my grandmother, the woman who had raised and protected me. I cried for the family I had lost as a child. I cried for all the things I now knew and wanted to forget. And finally, I cried for myself. Because somewhere along the way the child that I was just stopped existing and the woman I was now came into being.

The next day I got up very late. I told Jaime that if Francesca called not to pass the call to me. If she should insist he was to say I would not see her. I was running. I was running as quickly as I could. In a few days I would leave Spain and never come back. If I was lucky she would never find me and I might find some peace. If not, I might lose my sanity. In a few days, just a few more days, I would be free.

I met with the lawyers and explained that I wanted to liquidate all my assets. I told them that I would be leaving Spain within the week. They had been surprised but I would not be talked out of it. They tried to convince that it was a mistake that it would cost me a fortune. I had enough money for ten lifetimes; I needed my life. I needed to save what was left of me. After that the conversation was closed. I would not be persuaded.

†

I finished my breakfast on the terrace and afterward I just wandered around the house remembering my childhood there, saying my good-byes.

I lingered with memories and they led me to the library for a book that afternoon; my eyes noticed the purse I had left on top of the desk along with the envelope. I remembered the envelope and decided that it was time I read it. It wasn't going to get easier, so I might just as well read it. I wanted the memories to end; I wanted to wrap things up so that I might finally be free.

I opened the envelope and along with a letter was a diary. The letter began with:

My Dearest Granddaughter…

As my eyes scanned the words she had written my mind could not believe what they were reading. The words opened the door and the truth flooded my world with the force and the rage of a tsunami. I felt each assault and how it destroyed each compartment in my world that I had created. All the doors were opened. There was no hiding; there was no place left for me to go.

I still could not believe she had known is what kept going over and over again in my head. She had known all along what had happened. It was all there. And when I had read it all, the pages fell from my hands to the floor. She should have told me. I sat down slowly in shock and all I could say over and over again was "she should have told me."

The past came back with the force and unpredictability of a tidal wave. My eyes closed as a scream rose from within me and escaped my lips. "NO!!!!"

Excerpts from my mother's diary brought back the past with the reality and insight I had not been able to grasp as a child. It was the past my grandmother had tried to protect me from. It was a story within my own. And the puzzles started to form a tapestry with such complexity I did not want to see and could not escape.

"She had the measles and you left her to go on a shopping spree to Paris," he retaliated.

"Stefan, you're driving too fast!" Carlotta said as the Porsche took yet another sharp turn. *"Stefan, remember the girls are in the car, slow down!"* She was yelling now. María put her little hand in mine and squeezed hard.

"All right," Stefan answered, finally slowing down.

"You know María has a very sensitive stomach. If she gets sick we won't be going out tonight," Carlotta reminded Stefan.

He breathed hard in frustration.

"You're always overreacting with her. Cristina is your child too, you know," he added sarcastically.

"Cristina is stronger than María. Cristina can take care of herself."

"Cristina is just a child, Carlotta. She's only eight years old."

"I don't want to fight tonight, Stefan," she announced and stared out the window.

That was the signal my mother gave when the conversation was over. I had heard many fights like this. They were common to me. I always wondered why she didn't love me. I still wonder to this day. I needed her so much and she never seemed to notice. Not that my father was that loving either. When he referred to that trip to Paris he omitted that he had accompanied my mother.

The person that my sister and I truly felt loved by was Mother's mother. Grandmama spoiled us and truly made us feel wanted and welcomed when we would go and visit. We did not visit very often. My parents always had some other place that they wanted to be. I always wondered why they bothered to drag us along. In retrospect, I believe it was out of guilt. They must have loved us in their own way. I honestly believe that it was guilt and the knowledge of what would people say more than love. It is who they were; they never had a chance and neither did we.

Before we got back to the villa, Papa did speed up again and poor little María did get sick. He was furious that she had gotten sick in his car. When we pulled up the drive he hopped out of the car in disgust.

"Get her out of the car right now! It stinks in there!" he yelled at Mother.

At that moment, the front door opened and a young woman started walking toward the car. Mother went around to get María out of the car. Papa noticed the young woman right away and smiled. Mother was looking at Papa and her eyes followed his gaze. A smile appeared on her face as well.

"Stefan, this is Francesca, Victoria and Marcel's daughter," Mother told Papa. He walked up to the girl and kissed her on the cheek.

"Very lovely, very lovely indeed. Dios Mio, I remember you when you were a child and now you are a beautiful young woman," he said in the charming way he had. The girl blushed.

"She and Victoria will be here in France for the next few weeks. Perhaps we can take Francesca to Italy with us when we go next week," Mother suggested.

My father smiled and nodded his head.

Mama took María inside and Papa lingered outside. When I closed the car door he remembered my presence. He looked in my direction and I could see he resented my being there. Papa never lost an opportunity to flirt with the ladies. Oh, the ladies. I was in the way. This was to be his next conquest. I lowered my eyes and started walking toward the house.

"Are you Cristina?" the girl asked. I looked up and that was the first time I saw Francesca's smile. She knelt down in front of me and her hand went out to me. I put my hand in hers and nodded.

"Your grandmother has told me so much about you," she said sweetly.

I smiled into her beaming face.

I heard Papa clear his throat and looked up to see his frowning face. I pulled my hand away from her and walked toward the house. I had lunch alone since María had already been put to bed. She and I usually had our meals together. Mother and Father dined alone or usually with friends, but never with us.

After lunch I went into the garden to my favorite secret spot. It was in the loneliest part of the garden. I would sit under a beautiful big tree for hours and dream of a faraway world. I would always look up, wonder what it would be like to climb all the way to the top, and see the whole world from up there. I was not allowed to do such things like climbing trees. Mama always said, "young girls should be clean and tidy not dirty like those undesirable village children."

So, I would sit under my tree and look up and wonder. That's how Francesca found me that day.

"Hello Cristina," she said softly. I looked at her and was met again with a smile. "What are you doing here all alone?" she asked gently.

"This is my secret place," I said, giving her my only secret.

She looked all around her and then back toward me.

"Yes, it's a beautiful place." She sat down next to me. "This is a big tree. Have you ever tried climbing it?" As she asked, I immediately looked at her as if she knew what I had been thinking.

"I'm not allowed," I answered simply.

She looked suddenly sad. "Why?"

"Mama says I'm supposed to be a lady. Only peasants climb trees."

She looked at me tenderly and her hand caressed my cheek.

"I know where there is a bird's nest with little eggs. Would you like to see it?" I asked her enthusiastically.

She smiled and nodded her head.

We spent the afternoon exploring the garden and the woods around the villa. She was kinder to me in those few hours than my mother and father had been my whole life. We ran through the woods and played hide-and-seek. I loved being with her.

Late in the afternoon we started back to the house hand in hand. As we were coming toward the house my mother suddenly appeared and walked out to meet us.

She immediately noticed that I had gotten dirty. I recognized the look of disapproval in her eyes and my hand unconsciously squeezed Francesca's. She looked down at me and then to my mother.

"I'm sorry, Carlotta, if we stayed out too long, but I had such a lovely time exploring with Cristina. She is a lovely child, much like her mother." As she finished speaking Mother's face changed.

Mother smiled at Francesca. "I've been waiting to speak with you all afternoon," my mother said charmingly.

"Go and have your bath before dinner, Cristina dear," Mother said to me lovingly.

Francesca knelt down in front of me and took both my hands into hers. "Thank you for the loveliest afternoon I've ever had." She gave me a brilliant smile. She then leaned toward me and kissed my cheek. As she stood up again she released my hands, still smiling.

"Go on, Cristina," repeated Mother.

I walked toward the house. When I reached the door to go inside I looked back and saw mother holding Francesca's hand and kissing her on the cheek. Then they walked toward the gardens. I could hear my mother laughing as I went in the house.

Carlotta led Francesca away from the house. "I have been waiting for you all afternoon," she said softly as she pulled Francesca into an embrace.

"I'm sorry, I really enjoyed being with your daughter. She's very sweet," Francesca answered.

"If you like Cristina, just wait till you see María."

"Why do you always do that?" Francesca asked as she pulled away from her and started to pick a flower.

"What?" Carlotta asked, not understanding what she meant.

"Since I've known you, every time we discuss your daughter, Cristina, you tell me how much better María is." She still did not look directly at Carlotta.

Carlotta just stared at Francesca not saying anything else. After a few moments Francesca looked into the eyes of a woman who was wondering.

"Why, Carlotta?" she asked, looking straight into her eyes.

"You're imagining things," Carlotta looked away, suddenly nervous. Francesca started walking away from her toward the house.

"Where are you going?"

"You don't trust me!" Francesca turned to look at her.

"I don't know why I do it. She needs so much. She always has. María, well she just loves you back," she stated simply.

"Anyway, what does it matter? She doesn't care. All she ever does is go off and stare out into nothing. She is just like my father used to be."

"How can you be such a bitch with your own daughter?"

"Did you come here for her or for me?" Carlotta asked in anger.

"Shut up, Carlotta. Just shut up," Francesca said as she put her arms around her neck. She rubbed her body seductively against the older woman.

"God, you drive me crazy," Carlotta said as her lips descended upon Francesca's waiting mouth. The two women came back to the house from the gardens two hours later.

✝

The diary had begun to take on a life of its own. The pages seemed to come alive and the parts that were missing I simply filled in with my memory. I shut the book with such anger that it hurt my hands. They had been lovers…

"No! No! Why her? Of all the people in the world, why my mother?" I asked myself, closing my eyes tightly. But, still the tears came and rolled down my cheeks.

Is that why I was like I was? Did I want Francesca because my mother had been that way? I had never even looked at women before I had gone to New York. Did I want Francesca so badly because of what I was obviously exposed to or because I just liked women? I was so confused that I didn't know what to think or do anymore. I wasn't sure whether my actions were my own or brought out as retribution for what they had done to me. They had all lied to me. I hated them. I hated them all.

They had destroyed my childhood, and if that wasn't horrible enough they had made me love them all the while. I did love them. I had loved them all so much and they had hurt me. They had hurt me; but not only that, they had taken my sister from me. They had killed my sister. They had killed my sister? It was their fault!

I sat behind the desk for a long time, wrapped in a veil of confusion. A feeling of detachment started to take over once again. Oblivion, just existing without any feeling, was comforting. I could not bear another emotion. I could not bear any more. I was drowning as memories flooded my mind.

Suddenly I realized the room was dark and my attention was directed toward the ringing that had disturbed my state of non-movement. It was like being stuck on the pause button. The telephone, it was the telephone ringing that had brought me back.

I felt strangely alienated from my feelings and numbness overtook me. I saw my hand reaching for the telephone as if I was looking at the hand of another person. I put the receiver next to my ear and said hello in Spanish. *"Oigo?"* My voice sounded odd even to my ears. All I could think about was the fact that I felt nothing.

"Cristina?" The voice on the other end asked.

"Si."

"Cristina, thank God. I have been so worried. I need to see you. I'm coming over to you now. Can you hear me? Cristina, did you hear me? It's Francesca!"

"I know who you are," I said quite simply and without anger.

"What's wrong? I need to see you," her voice pleaded over the phone.

"My grandmother is dead. I'm tired now. I can't talk anymore."

As I was hanging up the telephone I could hear her yelling "Cristina!"

I opened the diary once more and began to read again.

†

"Annais, come into the water. It's deliciously warm," beckoned Carlotta.

"Later, not now," she answered as she walked over to where the two little girls were playing by the pool. As she approached, Cristina looked up and gave her a smile.

"Hi! What are you two doing?" she asked.

"We're coloring and then cutting out the figures. We want to do a collage for you," María answered with a smile.

María was a beautiful child. She reminded one of those beautiful children that painters of old would use as angels on their canvases. She was beautiful not only on the outside but she also possessed a beauty that only comes from within and it could be seen in every one of her smiles.

Annais looked down and saw a lot of different little cutouts, all colored brightly and lying all over the table.

"Why it's a lovely idea," she said to them.

"It was Cristina's idea to make it for you."

"Thank you," she said, looking down at the little girl who was smiling at her.

"You won't forget?" Cristina asked excitedly.

"No, little one, I won't forget." She lightly caressed the child's cheek as she walked back toward the pool.

"Annais, come on, jump in, the water is wonderful," Carlotta called to her again.

"I'm coming," she said, jumping into the water.

The children were called into lunch by their Nana. They were led into the kitchen where their lunch was waiting for them.

"Nana, my pictures! My pictures may be blown away! I left them on the table by the pool!" Cristina said excitedly and ran out the door and back into the garden toward the pool.

When she got there she did not see her mother or Annais. Most of her pictures were still on the table but some were scattered on the grass. She hurried to pick up all the ones that she saw. Some had been blown all the way toward the other side of the garden.

She went to pick them up and as she was picking up the small pieces of paper she heard voices nearby. As she raised her eyes she saw them. She became as still as a statue. Nothing could have prepared her to see her mother kissing Annais wantonly on the mouth and groping at her breast as she lay down on top of her in the grass.

She got up quickly, dropping all of her pictures on the ground and ran back to the kitchen.

"Cristina, your pictures? Did you find your pictures?" asked Nana.

"No," she answered in a very quiet voice as she picked up her soupspoon and started to eat her lunch.

†

I closed the book slowly, carefully put it in the drawer in front of me and shut it. I raised my eyes and as I did so the library door burst open. Francesca stood before me.

Jaime came in seconds behind her. "I'm sorry, miss. She just pushed by me, I couldn't stop her." As he spoke, I had gotten up and started walking toward her.

I stood silently in front of her for a brief moment. Then my hand went up to caress Francesca's cheek... The smell of her filled my senses, and as before, I could not walk away from her. I accepted that I would never be able to just walk away. My other hand went behind her neck and slowly I pulled her to me until my mouth met her lips. A stunned Jaime left the room in silence.

"I..." Francesca tried to say before my finger covered her mouth to silence her again.

As I pulled away she stood very still. My eyes searched her face and then my hands took on a life of their own as they traveled over her body. I needed to touch her, to feel her skin, smell her hair. I needed to taste her and hold her. I needed something that only she could give.

Francesca stood still, not understanding what was happening. She could see that my eyes had a faraway and detached look about them.

"What's wrong, *querida*?" she asked softly.

"I've missed you," I answered simply. "Come!" I grabbed Francesca by the hand and pulled her to follow me. We went out to the garden and were encompassed by the darkness outside.

"Cristina, it's too dark out now. We can't see anything out here. Let's go back inside." She pulled her hand away from my hold.

I turned to face her and Francesca could see my face from the light of the house behind her. "I want to show you a secret place." Suddenly the excitement left me and it was replaced by an overwhelming feeling of confusion.

Francesca stood very still.

"I...it wasn't here...it wasn't here." I said softly, looking out into the darkness and then back at Francesca.

My hand went up to touch my temple and my eyes closed briefly. I felt so tired, like the weight of the world was on my shoulders.

Francesca walked over to me, slowly put her hand around my waist and walked me back into the house.

"You're tired. Where is your room?"

I pointed toward the staircase and Francesca led me to it.

We went up the stairs in silence. When the door to my bedroom was closed behind us I turned and faced her.

"Run away," I said to her menacingly.

"I can't."

I had lost control. I felt nothing one moment and was filled with rage the next. I wasn't even sure where I was all the time anymore. Something was happening but I wasn't sure just what.

"I'm afraid," I whispered. "I don't understand what's happening to me. I'm scared, and I don't know what to do. Help me!" I cried, covering my face as I fell on my knees to the floor. "Help me? Oh God, please help me," I cried out.

I was filled with such loneliness. I was going to be in trouble. I knew I was.

"Mommy is going to be mad." I had seen them and I knew that Mommy was looking for me. "I won't tell. I promise I won't tell," I kept crying.

"Sweetheart, what are you talking about?" Francesca's arms embraced me.

"I won't tell. I promise I won't tell what you and Mommy were doing." As I finished saying this I felt her body tense up.

I kept crying. Mommy would find me and she would be mad. I hated her. She always took what I loved away. She would take Francesca away. I reached out for her. I held her hard and cried inconsolably.

"Don't be mad, Annais. I didn't mean to do anything bad. I was only looking for my pictures. I didn't mean to see you and Mommy," I choked out between tears. I looked up to her face.

She was looking down at me at first in surprise and then suddenly her eyes were filled with such sadness that tears welled up inside them and soon were rolling down her face.

"It will be all right, *querida*. I never knew you saw us. I'm so sorry. I'm so very sorry. I'll make it all right, I promise," she said tenderly.

My eyes were filled with love for her. She was going to make it all right; Mommy was not going to be mad. I put my face back on her chest.

We both sat on the floor. I held on to her as if hanging on to life, because, that is what she was and that is what she is still. I fell asleep as she stroked my hair.

Chapter Eleven

It felt cold. As I opened my eyes I realized I was on the floor in someone's arms. I looked up and saw that it was Francesca. She was asleep, holding me tightly against her with her back leaning against a chair. As I pulled away from her she awoke.

The room was filled with moonlight. I looked away and got up. My body felt stiff from having been on the floor. I was stretching and rubbing my shoulders with my back to her when I felt her hands begin to rub my back.

She massaged my shoulders and neck. She had always had the power to make my body come alive. I turned around to face her. I looked at her face carefully, as if by looking at her I would see something I needed to see.

I pulled her to me and my mouth sought to fill its hunger. My hands were harsh. I again was filled with the desire to love her and hurt her at the same time. She tried pulling away from me but I tore open her blouse in frustration and I could hear the buttons as they assaulted the wood floors. We stood staring at each other in surprise.

I took a step away. I didn't know what I was doing anymore. I no longer had the power to see the difference from what I wanted and what I should not want. She came over to me and walked me over to my bed.

"I'm tired, Francesca," I whispered to her in confusion. I wasn't sure of anything anymore. It was like my mind was filled with a fog I could not find my way out of and I was tired.

"I know...I know," she said as she undressed me slowly and put me to bed. After tucking me into bed she started toward the door.

"No! Don't leave me!" I cried out for her. She walked back and got into bed with me. "I'm afraid of the dark. You won't tell will you?"

She just stared at me for a long while and then held me very tightly to her.

"No. No, little one, I won't tell, it will be our secret." I smiled, went into her embrace and once again fell asleep in her arms.

†

After lunch I was put to bed for the traditional Spanish nap time. During this time I usually did everything except sleep. I waited for María to fall asleep, snuck out of our nursery and went out to the garden.

I went to my secret place. I stood in front of that huge tree and somehow I thought it mocked me. It stood there, daring me to climb it. I had always wanted to but Mother would have punished me if I were ever to get caught. I stared at it only a few more seconds before I started climbing that giant tree as fast as I could.

When I reached the top I saw another world. It all seemed so small from up there, not like when I was on the ground where everything was bigger than me, making me feel so insignificant. Up there it was all manageable.

I could see our house and the pool. I looked all around and for the first time in my life I felt such a sense of freedom as I never had or ever would feel again. I closed my eyes and took a long breath, and just smiled to myself and my newfound independence.

I just needed me. I opened my eyes and I could see my Nana looking around the garden calling out my name. Mother followed out behind her. She was angry. Mother's anger always meant pain in one way or another.

My newfound security became shaky and I started to quickly go down the tree. If she knew I had gone out that was one thing, I was already in trouble. But If she found out about the tree climbing...well, I wasn't sure what would happen, but with Mother it was better not to find out.

I was going down as quickly as I could and as I looked down I saw her down below. Francesca was looking up and smiling. I looked away and as I did my foot missed the branch and I felt myself falling through the air. All of a sudden the whole world went dark.

Through the mist that I found myself in I could hear her calling, "Tina! Tina!"

†

My eyes opened slowly and gradually they became accustomed to the darkness that surrounded me. I started to sit up and felt the tug of an arm around my waist. I looked over and saw Francesca's face on the pillow. She was asleep.

No matter how many times I started down one road somehow I always seemed to land in the same place. Memories long forgotten were flooding my mind at such a breakneck speed that sometimes I felt I was being drowned by them.

All the pieces were coming together and the picture they were creating was not something I wanted to see. Why? Why was this horrible nightmare slowly following me back to reality? That old dream suddenly came to mind.

I was running down a long corridor. I was so afraid. It was dark and my feet were wet. I remember voices calling my name and the fear. For that year that I did not speak after the accident I was consumed with that dream. Until one day it stopped and I started trying to remember or trying to forget. I'm not quite sure which anymore.

All I know is that Francesca was there, lying next to me. My past and my future lay in her. I was afraid of what I was going to remember. I couldn't seem to get the image of my mother and Francesca together out of my mind. I closed my eyes and let out a sigh. As I leaned back I felt her arm tighten around me and as my head found my pillow, Francesca found my shoulder to lay her face on.

I stroked her hair and buried my face into it and slowly breathed in the smell of it. I couldn't imagine my life without her in it and yet she had to be punished. Punished? Why did that idea come into my head? I didn't want to remember anymore! My arms went around her sleeping body and I pulled her closer to me.

✝

Her face hovered over me. I felt like a swimmer trying to swim up from the deep and awaiting me is her face. Somehow through the haze there was always Francesca's face.

"Tina! Tina!" She kept saying over and over again. My eyelids fluttered, trying to focus.

"My head hurts," I finally whispered.

"Oh, thank God, you're alive! Don't worry, little one, it will be okay. Stay still please." Her voice sounded far away but hearing it made me feel better.

I was taken by ambulance to a private clinic nearby. I could only make out muffled voices through the sound of the siren when the darkness overtook me once more.

I awoke in a strange room. It was all white and sterile looking. Later, I found out I had been in a coma for three days. I looked around and saw Mother and Francesca talking in the corner. They were whispering, but I could tell that they were arguing about something.

Annais turned to walk away when my mother grabbed her by the arm and pulled her back to her, kissing her on the mouth. She fought her only for a brief moment and then her arms went up around my mother's neck. All I could do was stare in silence. I turned my face away before they could see me. I could hear them whispering again before I fell asleep.

I stayed in the clinic for two weeks. I had suffered a concussion and had been in a coma for a few days. Other than that just some scratches and bruises, no broken bones.

The doctor told my mother to keep an eye on me and report any headaches or blackouts. I had been very quiet during my hospitalization, more than usual, staring into nothing for long periods of time. This seemed to upset my mother more than usual. The doctor still wanted to keep me under observation but mother argued that I would be more comfortable at home.

I would notice Francesca looking at me with concern in her eyes and I would look away. She had tried talking to me many times but I remained silent. Many nights she stayed in the hospital with me while my mother went home. Hers was the face I would see during the night, the one that gave me the glass of water, the one that helped the nurse change the sheets once when I had an accident during the first few nights.

She had comforted me and loved me. The first night I woke up in the middle of the night and called out, her voice was the one I heard in the dark.

"Mama!" I called out in fear. "Mama!"

"Shhhhh, little one. It's Annais. Mama is not here right now. Don't be afraid, everything will be all right." She spoke to me softly as her hand stroked my hair. I felt her lips kiss my forehead.

"You're going to be fine, but you have to try to keep still. Would you like some water?"

"Yes, please."

"Such a polite young lady you are. Your mother would be proud," she said half-jokingly. My eyes began to get accustomed to the darkness and I could see her walking toward a table and then walking back with a glass of water in her hand. She held my head up gently and I drank a little.

"Would you like to talk for a little while?" she asked.

"No," I said, turning my face away into the pillow.

I knew she stood motionless for a few seconds and then I heard her walk toward the other side of the room. I turned my face and I could see her sitting in a chair looking back at me.

"If you need me, I'll be here."

"I don't need you. I don't need anybody," I said to her harshly, tears welling up in my eyes.

A sob escaped me and she walked over to me. She lay down next to me and held me in a warm embrace. At first I tried pulling away from her, but gradually I didn't resist. On the contrary, my arms went around her neck and my face lay on her shoulder, half-buried in her neck. I felt safe with her. I felt safe and warm.

†

The light of day is what woke me. It rudely came through a crack in the heavy curtains and hit my face with its cruelty.

It awakened me to the fact that I was in my grandmother's house with Francesca in my bed. She was mine. After all these years she was still mine. No one would take her from me. If only I could keep the memories from taking over. I wasn't sure when they came just what I should do.

There were voices in my head. I had to shut out the voices in my head. I looked at Francesca as she slept. So beautiful. I had always thought her so beautiful. They thought she was beautiful too.

†

"Well, young lady, I think it's time you were going home," I heard someone say. I looked up to see my father standing in the doorway of my hospital room.

He walked over to Mother and they started talking about the arrangements of my coming home. I was to go to the villa and in a few days they would go to Italy as planned. María and I were to follow in a week or two. I just looked at them and said nothing.

As usual their plans would not be changed with the inconvenience of a child. Something must have shown in my face because when I looked in Annais's direction I saw pity in her eyes. I stared back at her in anger.

How dare she feel pity for me? I didn't want pity. Mother and Father walked out to speak with the doctor.

"You will be joining us soon in Italy," she said in a loving voice, trying to console me. She reached out her hand to console me but I pushed it away.

"Don't touch me!" I said to her. She stepped away from me in surprise. "I don't want to go to Italy! I don't want to see you anymore! Go away!" I yelled now.

Her eyes welled up with tears and she walked out of the room. I had hurt her and it felt good.

Of course, two weeks later, María and I joined them in Italy. As soon as we arrived I could sense that something was wrong.

You could feel it in the air. My parents appeared openly hostile to one another. And by this I mean more than the usual.

The first night after our arrival, as a special treat, we were allowed to have dinner with them. Right from the beginning, it became a battlefield. Sides had to be taken.

"Tomorrow I thought we could take the girls to see the countryside. Wouldn't you like that, Annais?" my father asked.

"Annais does not like the country," Mother stated flatly without even looking up from her dinner plate.

Father's face became furious but he didn't utter a word.

"I would like to go with the girls. Perhaps we could try?" Annais said, looking in Mother's direction.

Mother looked up and nodded her head but not too happily. It had been a concession and nothing more.

"Well, now that it's settled, how was your trip here, girls?" Papa said in his most charming voice. Papa could be very charming, and if truth be told, he had always been kinder to us than Mama. I don't know why they had children; I guess it was what was expected. Once I heard Papa say that it was necessary to pass on the family money.

"The train ride was wonderful, Papa," replied an excited María. She proceeded to describe the ride and how we had bought cotton candy from a concession stand on our arrival into Italy and how Marcel, our poodle, had tried to eat some and how he had gotten all sticky.

María was a charming child. Mother had been right about that. Everywhere she went she brought the sunshine with her. How could you not love her? And of course everyone did, especially me.

"And you, Cristina? Did you enjoy the trip?"
asked Papa.

"No, it's too hot here" I said to him. He looked
angry and turned to Annais.

"Well, you are going to love the countryside. It is
so beautiful to see the wildflowers. They are all in
bloom now, you know."

✝

Her eyes opened and she was looking at me
expectantly. Waiting to see something but she wasn't
sure quite what. I was propped on my elbow looking
at her as my hand stroked her hair.

"I was remembering how beautiful your hair
looks with wildflowers. Blue ones and yellow ones.
Italy has beautiful wildflowers. We should go there. I
remember..." My voice just kind of faded away.

I was lost somewhere. Neither here nor there.
Francesca touched my cheek and brought me back to
this reality. I looked at her in surprise. How had she
gotten into my bed?

I felt confused and disoriented and it must have
shown. I looked around trying to understand where I
was.

"Where are we?" I asked her.

She looked at me for a moment and very softly
caressed my face.

"We are up too early. Come let's go back to
sleep," she said as she gently pulled me into her
embrace and stroked my hair.

I pulled away from her. I sat up on the bed, trying to get a grip on my thoughts. They were going so fast all around me that I couldn't focus.

"Tina," she said, holding my arm.

I again pulled away from her.

"Don't touch me!" I said sharply. I looked down at her with the eyes of a stranger.

The sheet had slipped down to her waist. My eyes traveled to her breasts and my hands proceeded to fondle them. A moan escaped her lips and my mouth and my body covered her. At first she fought me but it was to no avail. She always surrendered in the end. I needed the taste of her skin. My hands touched her, aroused her, and finally I would go inside her and fill my hunger for her. I wanted the pleasure her body gave me. Why shouldn't I? She was mine! What hadn't I done to have her?

†

Two hours later we were still in bed. I held her tightly to me, my face in her hair as she spoke.

"Let's go home," she said.

"Home? Where is home?" I asked her. She turned toward me and looked into my eyes.

"Let's go back to St. Maarten, to my house," she pleaded with a smile on her lips; a smile that disappeared when she heard me speak.

"Why should I go anywhere with you?" I asked her cruelly.

"Because you love me...and I love you."

"When did I tell you I loved you?"

"That night...in the dark...in New York." Tears started streaming down her cheeks. My finger started wiping them away. My eyes were avoiding hers.

"Tina, please!" she pleaded, but upon hearing her pet name for me the anger within me took over. I grabbed her hair and pulled it tight.

"AHHH!!!" she cried out. I was hovering over her, ready to strike, much like a predator does with its victim.

"I don't love you!" I said to her between my teeth. My body was on top of hers, my hands pinning hers down.

"Don't do this, please!" she sobbed.

"I can do whatever I want!" I said menacingly. "Why would I love you?" I taunted her.

"Tina, please...don't do this, don't do this," she repeated as her tears became sobs. Her body shook with her pain. I could hear her pain as she cried.

My anger disappeared as quickly as it had come. Her tears had always had the capacity to move me. My lips kissed her face gently and then her eyes and finally her mouth.

"Don't cry," I begged her. "Please don't, don't cry," I whispered into her ear as my lips consoled her, covering her with soft kisses.

Her arms went around my neck and held me close. I rolled off her and half her body was on mine. I stroked her hair. "We'll go to St. Maarten for a while. It was very beautiful there. Would you like that?"

"Yes," she said as she looked down at me.

†

A few days later we arrived in St. Maarten. It was warm and lovely and best of all it had no memories of my past. For years I had longed to remember now I just longed to forget. Something was happening to me. Something I couldn't quite grasp. I knew I was losing a battle and I wasn't quite sure what it was. I just wasn't sure anymore. I wasn't sure of anything.

Chapter Twelve

The house in St. Maarten was finished and it was truly a dream house. It stood high on a cliff and the side that faced the ocean was made completely of glass. I stood there before the ocean and it suddenly dawned on me how vast the world really was, large enough for a person to be able to hide and never ever be found.

Perhaps it was possible to be happy still. The moment we left Spain I was able to breathe easier. I felt more in control of myself. I was able to take a deep breath and fill my lungs. Perhaps we could be happy here.

We had been on the island only a few days but I hadn't dreamed since our arrival. No more nightmares to confuse or torment me. For a brief moment in Spain I really thought I would go mad. I'm sure if I had stayed I would never be happy again. It was good here. There were no memories here to torment me. The past was where it should be, in the past. Francesca also seemed to find a new sense of freedom. We laughed more; we were happy, God we were so happy.

I didn't want any answers anymore. I just wanted to forget all I knew. The past that I used to search for

I now wanted to run from. There was something horrible there. I knew that now or, I should say, I felt it. Horror was the perfect word for it. I would never search again.

I had brought the diary with me. It was in my suitcase. I had stopped reading it the night Francesca arrived. And, at that moment, I knew I must never open it again.

I was pulled back into a soft embrace. She stood behind me holding me close to her. I could feel the warmth of her breath on my ear as she spoke softly to me.

"I love you," she whispered into my hair.

"Mmmm…you feel good." I leaned back against her. "I like it here. It's like a different world. Away from everything and everyone."

"It is. It's our world, yours and mine," she said softly as we both looked out into the ocean.

Yes, it was our world. And yes, it was beautiful. If only it could have remained that way. That moment was the only moment in my life that I was one with all. At that moment I had no past and no future. I just accepted and existed.

A few days later I was impatiently waiting for her; Francesca was never on time and I laughed at the thought

"Francesca, come on!" I shouted from the courtyard. "We are going to be late! Please hurry!"

"Okay, okay, I'm coming," she answered as she came down the staircase with a big smile on her face.

"What? What?"

"Did I tell you how beautiful you are today?' she said softly as she stopped in front of me.

I smiled as she put her arms around my neck and pulled me to her.

"It is very hard to stay angry with you," I said as I buried my face in her hair.

Francesca was my days and my nights. It was a fact in my life. She was all that happiness meant to me. I would die without her. It was that simple.

We had scheduled court time that morning at the club. We had both taken to going regularly and playing tennis there at least three times a week. Slowly we were creating our own world. No old memories, just concentrating on making new ones. I should have known it would never last. And God, how I needed it to. I had never felt this whole. I never would again.

We walked hand in hand on the beach at night and woke up in each other's arms in our bed in the morning. She loved and pampered me. She made all the pain of those years without her bearable. I needed her like a drowning man needs breath. I hungered for her and she fed and quenched it.

It was a day in the sunshine like so many before it. We had just finished our tennis game and I had gone ahead to order our drinks at the bar. I was happy. God, I was happy. My paradise came to a screeching halt.

"Cristina!" A voice called out to me.

I turned around and before me was Elena. At that moment my past collided with my present. I froze. I felt so cold. Instantly I felt a deadly chill fill my body.

"Cristina, it's wonderful to see you." Elena hugged and kissed me on the cheek.

"Hello, Elena," I managed to whisper.

"I was sorry to hear about your grandmother," she said sadly. "She was a tough one but she did love you."

"Thank you," I said to her.

"Since when have you been here?" she asked. "None of your old friends knew where you disappeared to."

"I have been traveling…" I trailed off. I felt the nausea coming. I felt dizzy and cold.

"Are you all right?" asked Elena, concerned.

"Yes," I said as I reached for the nearest chair for support.

"Here, let me help you. Do you want me to get a doctor?" She helped me sit down.

"No…I'm fine." I started to relax.

She sat next to me. "Are you sure you're okay?"

"Yes, really," I answered as my hand touched my hot cheek. I felt an immediate rush of fear. I had to run. "I have to go, Elena." I got up and started walking.

I remember her calling my name and I started to run. I ran and ran until I could not run anymore. It had gotten late. Suddenly I realized it had gotten dark. I was sitting on a bench facing the dark water of the ocean. How long I sat there, I don't know. I could not even remember how I had gotten to this place. I was tired. I felt so very tired.

✝

I closed my eyes and I saw her. "María!"

"Come on, Cristina, catch me!" She ran as I tried to catch her.

We were running in the garden. It was warm and the air smelled sweet with Mommy's roses.

"You can't catch me! You can't catch me!" We ran in sweet abandonment.

The air was filled with laughter. I kept letting her escape me.

"María, María, come here," Mommy yelled.

Suddenly we both stopped running and the laughter stopped.

"Come here, María. We are going into town with your father," Mommy said.

"No!" I yelled.

✝

My eyes shot open. I sat there listening to the sounds of the ocean that were no longer soothing. My past, my past was coming for me. Now that it had found me I would not be able to hide from it anymore.

I got up and started to walk. There was only one place for me to walk to.

123

†

"Where have you been?" Francesca yelled as I walked in. "I have been worried sick!"

I had just walked in front of the wall of glass without saying a word. I looked out to that ocean that only a few hours ago had given me such peace and all I saw was black water.

"I ran into Elena at the club," I remember saying. Was that me? Was that my voice? It sounded distant. The sound of it only made me feel colder. I remember wrapping my hands around my body and I fell on my knees to the floor.

Francesca was at my side immediately. I felt her embrace before she reached me.

"I can't escape them, Francesca, I can't escape them," I said as I lost consciousness.

†

"No! I don't believe you! I don't believe you!" I yelled. That day I ran too. I ran and ran.

"Querida," my grandmama said sweetly.

She had found me under the tree. I was huddled into a ball. I looked at her and buried myself in her embrace.

"Querida, es verdad, tu hermanita está con Dios," she whispered to me as she caressed my hair.

My sister was with God she told me.

I did not speak after that. The words just left me.

†

I swam up from the darkness that was both my friend and my enemy. The darkness and I were old friends. My eyes fluttered open and I seemed to be swimming through a sea of shadows. In front of me was a glimmer of light and I went toward it.

The room was filled with sunshine as I woke. My heart was pounding and my body felt winded and off somehow. I felt as if on a roller coaster; I felt unsteady and breathless. And the cruel reality of the real world had shown its specter and I could not run. I shook my head trying to somehow make it go away. I wanted to go back. Back to how I had felt on the island with Francesca

I could no longer deal with the inconsistency of my life. In one moment, in one swift moment, Elena had reminded me of what I was running from and now the past was here. It was here and I no longer could control it. It was coming at me like a wolf whose hunger must be fed.

I could no longer keep my eyes closed. As I opened them she was the first thing I saw. My Francesca, It had always been my Francesca.

"Hello." There was so much love in her eyes.

"Hello," I replied.

Her eyes. I could always just disappear in her eyes. I reached out and my fingers lightly caressed her face. Was she real? I couldn't tell what was real anymore. I was changing. Was it like this? Did it happen like this? Is this what it was like to lose your sanity? Death seemed a more peaceful way. Yes, in death there was no thought involved; hopefully things would just stop. Yes, death was definitely better.

"Hello, my love," she said softly as her lips kissed my temple. Her other hand caressed my face and I leaned into it.

"I love you, Francesca," I said simply as I looked up to meet her eyes. What I saw looking back at me were two beautiful eyes filled with a look of such tenderness that it took me by surprise. Her eyes filled with tears and they spilled over her cheeks.

"I hope you always do," she replied sadly, her head bent down.

"Yes, I always will."

She looked up again.

"I have always loved you." As I said this to her I sat up and lay my cheek on her breast. Her hand caressed my hair gently and we just sat there in each other's embrace.

Chapter Thirteen

We stopped going to the club and stayed mostly in the confines of the house. It wasn't that we talked about doing this; we just did. We were becoming good at escaping things. As to how long we could keep it going we didn't know. I took to taking long walks on the beach as Francesca watched me from the wall of glass above. The days were growing short. A part of me knew the end was near.

One afternoon I came in from my walk on the beach and heard loud voices coming from the drawing room. I walked toward them. The doors that were usually open to allow the flow of air and sun were closed. I could hear Francesca speaking as I opened the doors and walked in.

Elena was sitting on the sofa. She seemed upset. As I walked into the room she stood up and walked toward me.

"Cristina..." she started to say when Francesca interrupted.

"Cristina, Elena made some inquiries at the club and they directed her here."

"Cristina, I need to speak with you! What is going on here?" she asked, looking back at Francesca, who was looking at me.

"What can you possibly mean, Elena?" I asked as I walked to stand in front of the glass wall. As I looked out to the ocean I realized sadly it no longer gave me comfort. I had become a stranger to it.

"I have heard some really incredible rumors at the club," she finished in a barely audible whisper.

"And what have you heard, Elena?" I asked in a mocking voice, still looking out, pleading to my ocean to take me back. If I could only feel a part of it I could be happy again. I knew that. Why could I no longer feel that peace anymore?

"Cristina..." She started walking toward me.

I turned and was a mere few feet from her now. "And what have you heard, Elena?" I asked again.

She seemed uncomfortable, looking at Francesca and then back to me.

"Francesca, will you excuse us a moment please?" I asked and was met with hurt-filled eyes. She said nothing as she walked out of the room and closed the doors behind her.

As soon as Francesca left the room Elena started her attack.

"Cristina, do you know what they are saying? My God, you have to leave here!"

My eyes were still looking at the closed doors. I had hurt her by asking her to leave. It seemed that I was always hurting her. It seemed like another lifetime that I wanted to punish her for something. Somehow that didn't seem right anymore. Nothing seemed as I thought it should. And all I could do was stare at the closed doors and remember how hurt she had seemed when I asked her to leave us.

"Cristina!"

I looked back at Elena again and walked to the other side of the room to put some distance between us.

"Cristina, Come back with me. You can stay with me and Alfonso, if you wish to remain here for a while longer, but you must leave here before these rumors are heard and spread."

I looked out to the ocean yet again as my plea went still unanswered. And it was with a tired sadness that I spoke to Elena. "And what are they saying, Elena?" I asked as I ran a hand through my hair.

"That you and…that you and Francesca are more than friends." She was unable to look me in the eye.

I said nothing. I waited for her to speak again. I wasn't going to make this any easier for her.

"Cristina! Do you know what they are saying?"

"No, what are they saying, Elena?" I asked in a whisper. As the silence lengthened I looked in her direction and finally she looked up straight into my eyes.

"That you and Francesca are lovers. That you have been seen kissing on the beach. That you have been seen nude in the water fondling each other, that...Cristina, you can't stay here!" Again her eyes avoided meeting mine. I looked out at the ocean again.

"Is that what they are saying?" I asked disinterested.

"Do you understand the ramifications? Do you? Look at me!" she blurted out in anger. She took my arm and turned me around to face her.

"Elena, what would you have me do?" I asked quite unflustered.

"Leave here to start with. You come from an old family, Cristina. This is an added scandal that you don't need," she finished saying.

That got my attention. She knew something. It had never even occurred to me that she knew anything.

"What are you talking about, Elena? What do you know?" Now I sounded upset.

She moved nervously away, toward the middle of the room. "I...I just don't want to see you get hurt."

"Don't lie to me, Elena. You started this. Tell me, what scandals are you talking about?" I demanded.

"Cristina..." she left the sentence unfinished.

"You think I don't know? I know everything. I know more than I want to. I want to die because I don't think I can bear another day knowing." I was yelling now.

"Cristina, please," she said softly, walking back toward me.

"Get out, Elena!" She froze on the spot. "Get out! Your being here hurts me! Get out, please!" I cried out in pain. "GET OUT!!!" I shouted. She turned around and ran out of the room.

After a few minutes I ran to find Francesca. I knew instinctively that she would be in our bedroom.

I remember slamming the door hard. She stood near the bed in silence. I was breathless and started pacing. I felt the weight of my guilt and it was going to kill me. She remained silent. I suddenly stopped and turned to look at her.

I had done so much to have her. So much that I could not admit even to myself. She was more than love; she was my obsession. She always had been. I thought I was the one captured in this thing we had between us. But, at that moment I realized I had never been the victim. I had always known what I wanted and pursued and took. Francesca just loved. I felt like I had been used in so many ways and it was not that way at all. It had always been that way. WE, THE ALCALÁS, WE were the users. We took and took and never cared what remained in the aftermath.

I had hated them for so long—my parents. I had hated them and I was just like them. But not quite like them. I was the truest Alcalá of all.

I wanted Francesca. I had always wanted Francesca. And with that thought. I went to take what I wanted. Before she even had a chance to say a word my mouth covered hers.

My hands traveled up and down her body. I need to touch her with an urgency that even I didn't understand. And in my frustration I started ripping at her clothes. I wanted her skin, her smell, all that Francesca was. I wanted to possess and adore her.

As always she understood and quenched my needs and didn't fight me, but today even my hunger would surprise her. Within moments I felt the warmth of her flesh. We fell on the bed and I was above her. I felt and was consumed with the heat of desire and that was all that mattered. It had been so long since I had taken her like this.

My mouth searched for her breast and sucked it hard. I could feel the groan rising from my throat before I heard it. I was filled with a desire that only her body could quench. I teased and teased her. Her breasts were my torment so I made them her torment. I teased them with my teeth and then my tongue. Her back arched to give me more. I ached with a need to possess and my hand traveled lower to take her. I needed. I needed, that is all I knew.

Yes, she was so willing. She was ready for me and, quite suddenly, without her even realizing it, I was inside her. This was our dance. A dance of my possession. Because she was mine. As her hips started to buck I pressed harder. I could feel the orgasms, one after the other, wash over both of us. Her hands pulled at my hair in pleasure and also with a plea. I fell over her and I also tried reaching for breath.

But the hunger would not leave me. I could feel the fire burning behind my eyes. And when my eyes looked into hers all she saw was lust and it frightened her. I lowered myself between her legs never releasing her eyes from mine.

Then, just as quickly, I released her and my eyes saw what was my objective. She was so inviting. I closed my eyes and took in her scent and my mouth took and fed on her until her screams begged for my mercy. I did not hear; I did not want to. I took and I took until I had my fill. It had always been this way. I took her again and again. And in the end my body's exhaustion is what stopped me. Because in my mind I wanted her still. I would die wanting her.

She was mine.

When she woke up the next morning she woke up in an empty bed.

†

I walked on the beach. The water rushed up and hit my feet and all I remember seeing was water and sky. It was so peaceful. I felt one with the ocean again. My mind was so clear. Once I stopped fighting it all seemed so easy as to what I had to do. And I felt at peace.

Sunrises were always so beautiful. I wanted to see this one. This would be the most important one. The sky was filled with the magic of gold and as I held my breath waiting to see the first sparks of the sun I felt arms come around me from behind. I leaned back against her and we welcomed it together. My Francesca. My beautiful love, for that is who she was. She was love. That morning we welcomed the dawn together.

I left her two days later without a word. I took a plane back to Spain.

Chapter Fourteen

It was a long flight, but somehow all I remember was getting on and off a plane and on again. And all that was in my thoughts were thoughts of Francesca. My love. For that is what she always was: my love. I had run from her so many times. Run away; run as fast as my mind could take me only to go back to her. Finally, it was all so clear.

All those lonely years without her. Remembering only that I had to remember. Remembering and then wanting to forget. There is so much I regret. So much.

And of course there is now. Now I know and remember everything. And I know what I must do. I am an Alcalá, after all. I always have been. That is what I cannot run away from.

She knew. She had always known, my grandmama. She had guarded her secret and it killed her. Yes, it killed her.

And now, all I have before me are the realities I had never wanted to see and will no longer deny.

I am here now. In front of this ugly building. And I am getting out of this cab and I walk in knowing that this is something that I must do and even now— God forgive me—Francesca is all I think of.

"Come this way, Miss Alcalá," the nun said to me. "Please follow me."

I follow her down a long corridor and as she opens a door, I step inside.

"I will leave you with her," she says and I am left alone in a room with a bed and a young woman on it.

I walk closer to get a good view of her. It is all quite sunny and I can smell the sterility of the room. All the walls are painted a pristine white. No pictures or family photos to tell of her life. Just the sound from the machines. The machines that make her chest go up and down. I walk yet closer to have a better look, and as my eyes close I see her.

I see her when she was small and beautiful. I see her when she was full of life. When she was just my María. I remember that day...

"Come on, Cristina, catch me, catch me." And I ran after her through the trees. And all that I could hear was her laughter.

I open my eyes and I don't see that little girl in her face. As I feel the tears roll down my face I know it is my fault that she is here. And after all this I still want Francesca. She is the thought that never leaves me.

"María?" I hear myself say. I reach my hand out to touch her but I can't and I run out of the room. I run out of that ugly building. I get into the cab that is waiting. I can't stop the pain from bending me over with grief.

My beautiful María. I had done this to her. If I didn't end this madness I would hurt Francesca. I knew I would. And that I could not bear. I could not bear to know that someday I could be responsible for yet another tragedy.

I feel tired. I am now in the present and quite aware of my life. I feel the seed growing every day inside me. And I also know that it must end with me. The Alcalá curse must stop with me. I will face it all today. Grandmama had always known. She knew that someday I would have to face this.

I give the driver another address. This is an older place. Not as frequented. Out of town. It is a place that is to be kept out of sight. After all, who wants to be reminded of these people? Again I get out of the cab and I am shown to yet another room. This time I see an old man. A very old man tied down to his bed. In the distance I hear screams. But they don't frighten me. I have known and heard them my whole life.

Yes, I can see the resemblance. It is still there. I remember seeing him in Grandmama's old photos. I have his eyes. Yes, I have his eyes. I remember her telling me that I had his eyes. And now I also remember the sadness in hers when she said this to me.

This had been one of her secrets. This poor old man lying on this bed, with my eyes, looking at nothing, and just waiting to come back from the nothing.

Here was the man my grandmama had loved till her last breath. That day, that horrible day that she died, she had told me all about him. That day, that horrible day, I knew what I would become. Here he lay, bound to this bed. Here he had been for the last thirty years. Here in this hospital for the insane.

They told me that he'd had a quiet day and that he sometimes just lay there and stared out into the nothing. Apparently the day before he had attacked a fellow patient and had to be restrained. I thanked the doctor and left.

And now, my love, I come to you. I know that I must end this. I must end this before I am like him. Because that is what will become of me someday. I am no longer denying what will be. I must end this before I do more damage. How can I make you understand? Because I know I must make you understand, Francesca, my love.

Yes, my love. You. You, who have been the only real thing in my life; you, who gave me a purpose for living. I know what I feel now is the reality I have never wanted to face. And yet face it I must, if I am to save you. Yes, my love. I must save you from me. I must save you from me.

And so, I wait here for you. Because I know you will come. I know you will find me. I am as consumed with you as you are with me. But even so, you are different. You do not carry this seed inside you. It hurts me to know that in order to make you understand I must tell you the truth. Because the truth will be painful, my love. The truth will be painful.

As if in a book I turn this last page and you are here. I open the door and you are here before me. So beautiful. How could I have forgotten you all those years ago? I walk into your embrace and breathe you inside me with a sadness that I know is a good-bye.

"Cristina." Your voice is but a whisper. You follow me into the room and you are angry.

"Why did you leave? This has to end."

"I know," I whisper. All I can do is look at you as my vision blurs.

"Why are you crying? I am not angry. Yes, I am angry. You cannot just leave me like that." Your hand reaches out to caress my cheek.

"I'm sorry…" I can't speak anymore and the tears just come.

You take me into your embrace and I cry. I cry for you. I have always cried for you. This must end, my love.

You try holding on to me but I pull away. I must pull away from you because if I don't I know that I will never be able to release you. If I stay in your embrace I will not be able to ever let you go again.

"Francesca, my love, yes, you are right. This has to end. I can't go on with this any longer." My back is to you because I am afraid that my resolve will waver if I look into your eyes. So I go on.

"I remember everything, you see. I remember Mama and you. I remember Papa. I remember the day that started me on this road to madness. I killed them."

I now face you with eyes boiling over with tears. You take a step toward me and I take one away; keeping the distance between us.

"Tina?" I hear the tears in your voice. And I run to you. I run into your arms and hold on tight. One last time. I had to.

"I heard Mama talking to you that night. She was taking you away."

"Oh Tina?" you say as you cry and hold me tighter.

"I heard her. I couldn't let her do that. I couldn't. So I told Papa. He was so angry...and then things just started going crazy. Maria snuck in the backseat of the car. We were playing hide- and-seek. I saw them."

I felt the moment you suddenly became very still. I look up into your eyes and see the horror.

I step away from your embrace. While you remain a statue in shock, I keep on talking. I have to end this madness tonight if there is to be a chance to save you. To save you from the one that loves you. To save you from me, my love. To save you from me...

"She knew too." I see the question in your eyes as I say this. "Grandmama...she knew all along. That day, when she told me about María, I told her. I don't know why I forgot it all, but I did. Guilt hides the truth, I guess," I say softly. "I was always filled with a desire to remember, and I now know that what I wanted to remember was you."

Upon my saying this our eyes meet and I continue. "I have always loved you...even then. She was going to take you from me. So I told Papa." I was quiet for a bit.

I suppose I wanted to avoid the telling of this story. I wanted just a little longer with you. I take a deep breath and I know I must continue. "Before I knew it, the past just started pouring back. That night in the dark, in New York, remember?"

"Yes, you said you loved me," you say softly.

"Yes," I respond as I look at you. My Francesca. "That night I remembered it all. I thought I would go crazy. I had wanted to remember and then all I wanted was to forget. Then the call that Grandmama was sick..." I trail off.

"Abuela, estoy aquí." I am here, Grandmama.

"Cristina, mi vida, tienes que saber, tengo que decirtelo antes de morirme." She had something to tell me before she died.

"I remember being with her at her death bed. The things she said to me...she asked me to give you up."

I look at you and all I see are questions.

"I couldn't do that. I couldn't all those years ago either. She would make me give you up, she said. That's when I knew I had to stop her you see." As I look at you I see horror in your eyes yet again.

"Don't look at me like that, Francesca, I had to!" I scream.

You look horrified. "What did you do, Tina? Oh God, what did you do?"

"I had to stop her. She was going to take you away from me. She said I had to leave you before I ended up like my grandpapa. I had to, don't you see?"

I look at you and you just stare. So I continue.

"I kissed her and I put a pillow over her face. She was so tired, Francesca. And I wanted her to rest. Her burden was so great. She had kept the secret of María for so long to protect me. She had the secret of my grandpapa. She loved me she said, and she was cursed to see that same seed grow inside me as it had grown inside the man she loved. She looked so tired, Francesca. I wanted to help her sleep, you do understand, don't you?"

"Tina…" you whisper as you cover your face.

"She was so tired." As I finish saying this you look up and our eyes meet once more.

"I love you, Francesca. I have always loved you." With eyes filled with tears you open your arms to me. My love. You have always been my love. This is the image I want to take with me. I need the image of your face. I want to keep one lucid moment for you.

As I remember what I must do, I hold you close and take you inside me for the last time. Your embrace. That is what I want to take with me. The memory of your embrace and then I will set you free. Free from me and mine forever.

I tear myself away from you and as I walk away I can still hear you weeping. But soon I will set you free. I open the drawer and my hand reaches in. I feel the gun before I can see it. I take it out slowly and raise it to my temple. And then I hear the loud noise as I see the room turn and I am in your arms again.

†

Slowly both fell to the floor. Francesca held her tightly, never for one moment releasing her eyes. They were clear now. Finally free of the nightmare that had tormented her for so many years, a torment that she was partially responsible for. Cristina was dying. They were both now seated on the floor and Cristina lay partially on her lap, being held by her still. Tears slid down Francesca's cheeks. Cristina was just looking at her.

"Don't cry," she said softly as tears welled up in her own eyes.

"I won't," Francesca replied softly, giving her a smile.

"The only real thing in my life has been you," she said sadly.

"I'm so sorry I hurt you." Tears rolled down Francesca's face now.

"No, I came alive because of you. No one ever noticed me before you. I had the strength to be myself because of you. Loving you has been the only good thing in my life." As she finished saying this she gasped for breath.

"Don't leave me!" pleaded Francesca in a voice filled with agony.

"I can't stay," Cristina whispered sadly.

"I know," said Francesca, overcome with sadness. She kissed Cristina's forehead and then kissed her lips lightly. In the kiss, as they tasted each other's tears, she felt the moment that Cristina left her.

"No! Oh no!" she wailed as she held Cristina tightly to her chest. "AHHHHHHH!!!!" She cried out as she looked up in pain.

It was over. At that moment she knew she could not go on without her. Cristina was waiting. Cristina had always been waiting. She would go to her. They would be together forever. She raised the gun to her temple. Now they would both be free.

There was a loud explosive sound and all that followed was silence.

"Francesca?"

"Yes, my love?"

"Forever now?"

"Yes, forever and ever together now, my love."

Epilogue

AP WIRE…NEWS FLASH HEADLINES

September 22nd 2005 9:15AM

HEADLINES

DOUBLE DEATH--ANOTHER ALCALA
SCANDAL

THE SPANISH ROYAL CROWN-NO COMMENT

✝

"Isn't it horrible?" Elena heard the waitress comment.

"Yes, horrible."

"Such a tragic family. I read the whole story."

Elena kept looking down at the newspaper so the waitress went on.

"It seems the police are looking for people that might know something. First, the scandal about how the parents died almost fifteen years back and now the only remaining daughter was found shot under questionable circumstances."

"Yes, very questionable."

"She used to come in here sometimes, you know," said the waitress to impress her. "She was a nice customer. I remember she was a good tipper. You look like someone she came in with once..."

"No, I didn't know her," Elena replied.

"How awful. Such a well-known family to have been destroyed with such tragedy. Apparently, the Alcalá girl had a questionable reputation and was found shot in the arms of a woman who shot herself as well. You know, these women who like girls...who can understand these people."

"Yes..."

"Born to such wealth...they have fantastic lives. It isn't as if they ever lack for anything. I mean, these people have it all. Oh well, what can you do? Got to get to work. What will you have, miss?"

"Coffee, just coffee," Elena says.

The waitress leaves to get the coffee and Elena looks up finally and she remembers.

When her coffee arrives she opens a book that Cristina must have mailed to her a few days before the tragedy. She opens the book where the marker beckons and sees a poem titled *La Neblina*, or The Fog...

On top of the page the words written are: For clarity Elena... Cristina

The Fog
By S. Anne Gardner

Your eyes are closed to me now

just as my heart is closed to you.
A veil separates us...clear and copious like that fog that can be seen and not touched.
And still I stare into it...
Yearning...
not quite knowing for what
...but perhaps just for a shadow of you.

And in one instant,
I am filled with a sweetness of a summer's day,
The buzzing of the bees in a sea of green and the caress of the breeze

like being in a cloud, weightless...
Held in a warmth felt long ago and long forgotten
Surrounded by a perfume that filled all of me, it was familiar
Like a lost wanderer my eyes were slowly opened and in the fog
The vision was less shadow

The warmth of her touch was hypnotic and I was lost
Lost in the colors, in the rhythm, in the beauty of her and for one instant I thought the brightness...
She was the Sun
the sun whose kisses on my skin could burn...
and the lulling sound of the buzzing bees was hypnotic

And again the darkness cradled me
An old friend...in its gentle arms I sought oblivion
All I wanted was to rest and surrender;
to drown in the security of its familiarity and its nightmare

I lost myself in the arguing, the words...
I lost all the arguments that were never truly real.
I lost hold of what had kept me asleep for so many years.
I lost...

Each breath I took resonated in my ears like an avalanche
Lost in a sea of something foreign
Running toward an abyss
Endless in the wanting and...
Lost in its wake.

Walk with me, stroll with me through this garden.
Hold my hand and keep it close to your heart.
And the colors filled my senses but the fog had never been far behind me.

Memories that do not seize invade and I...
I reach for you and the image wavers
And something inside me knows
I will never touch you.

And as the fog comes so does the sunrise.
In the light of day your hand is in mine
And I am alive...I am finally alive.

And in the light of day I walk with her; her hand in mine.
Forever mine. . .

About the Author

S. Anne Gardner

S. Anne Gardner has lived all over the world and is now living on the East Coast of the United States. She has a love that fills her heart and children who fill her life. She has many interests and is a published author as well as a published poet. She enjoys sailing, horseback riding, art, traveling, reading, and writing. Her family, her friends, and her music fill her life in a world that is her own.

Books from Affinity eBook Press

Beginning of the End—Alane Hotchkin What happens when life doesn't go exactly as you planned and you must protect others from your own fate? Escaping a horrific childhood, Nikki longed to find happily ever after in adulthood. What she found was Hell. Or did it find her? Finding the courage to break the cycle of betrayal, she opens her heart one last time. Alex lived a childhood others dreamed of. Her father never once denied the young rebel a thing. All her life she dreamed of protecting others; to follow in her father's footsteps. Soon though she learned sex and fists made the most powerful of weapons. Alex controls the women in her life through fear and sex, will breaking the cycle be too much to overcome? Will loving Nikki be enough to change her, or is Alex beyond help?

Alex would give Nikki the world, but at what price? When a person's tightly controlled reality snaps what then…? This is the Beginning of the End for one of them and the ultimate sacrifice for the other. But who is who in this game of life?

Galveston 1900: Swept Away—Linda Crist On September 7-8, 1900, the island of Galveston, Texas, was destroyed by a hurricane, or 'tropical cyclone', as it was called in those days. This story is a fictional account of Mattie and Rachel, two women who lived there, and their lives during the time of the 'great storm'. Forced to flee from her family at a young age, Rachel Travis finds a home and livelihood on the island of Galveston. Independent, friendly, and yet often lonely, only one other person knows the dark secret that haunts her. Madeline "Mattie" Crockett is trapped in a loveless marriage, convinced that her fate is sealed. She never dares to dream of true happiness, until Rachel Travis comes walking into her life. As emotions come to light, the storm of Mattie's marriage converges with the very real hurricane. Can they survive, and build the life they both dream of?

This second edition of one of Linda Crist's best-loved novels maintains the original story, while incorporating some reader-pleasing passages that were cut from the first edition. As an added bonus, the short story "Something to Celebrate" is included at the end of the novel, detailing further adventures of Rachel and Mattie.

Rapture: Sins of the Sinners—A. C. Henley & Fran Heckrotte A serial killer is targeting young lesbians throughout the state of Texas. Texas Ranger Cochetta Lovejoy is assigned to the case. Convinced she knows who is committing the murders, Ranger

Lovejoy is willing to do whatever it takes to put the perpetrator behind bars--even if it means stretching the limits of the law by manipulating the judicial system. Detective Agnes Kelly-Elliott is one of Ft. Worth Police Department's finest investigators. When Ranger Lovejoy appears on the crime scene of a recent murder, Agnes fears a dark secret that, if revealed, could destroy her family ties, and end her career. This is a dark, gritty, graphic tale of desire gone awry, and flawed characters looking for redemption in all the wrong places.

Till There Was You—S. Anne Gardner Julia is a woman used to power and is not afraid to use it or impose her will to get her way. She appears to have the world but a part of her is empty and cold as a frozen tundra. Julia rides in the mornings to clear her head and to make plans for what she is about to set in motion. Theodora, known as Teddy, is trying to put together a marriage filled with uncertainties. She felt once upon a time that she would have a great love but that has eluded her. One morning these two women meet and from the first instance, it is explosive. The attraction is undeniable, the fears very real and the end without question will change them both forever.

Denial—Jackie Kennedy Time spent in Somalia has Doctor Celeste Cameron accustomed to living and working in a war zone. Coming back home to America, Celeste is glad to see the end of the peril she has been in—or so she thinks. Danger seems to follow Celeste and she finds it in the shape of Amy. What Celeste feels for Amy scares her more than anything she has faced in war zones. Amy has the same feelings, but is in denial and vows to marry Josh, Celeste's twin brother, no matter what. When fate brings them together again, will they give in to their mutual attraction or will they once again deny what they feel.

In Name Only—JM Dragon—Sequel to The Fix-it Girl Can an agreement forged out of necessity actually work?

'55 Ford—Erin O'Reilly Andrea McBride, the author of four books, wants to find someone to restore an old '55 Ford truck that she inherited in a real estate purchase. She will only settle for the best and finds RJ Whittaker who many proclaim to be the best restorer among millions.

An Affair of Love—S. Anne Gardner From a dark past, a forbidden love, a secret comes. Among the confusion and the chaos of an unwanted reality, two women find something they neither want nor can deny.

Desert Heat—Dannie Marsden For Luce Diamond, an undercover policewoman, her life is in shambles. Her longtime lover left her and an automobile accident that resulted in a child's death haunts her.

Taming the Wolff—Del Robertson ONLY ONE WOMAN...HAS THE POWER...TO TAME THE WOLFF...

Private Dancer—TJ Vertigo Reece Corbett grew up on the mean streets on New York City, abused, used and in trouble with the law. Faith Ashford grew up wealthy, with all the creature comforts that money provides. When they meet fireworks begin.

Miriam and Esther—Sherry Barker Miriam thought her life would play out in the bustling metropolis of Dallas, but after a life-changing accident, she moves to the small town of Cool Lake, Texas to get her head on straight and regain her senses.

McKee—A.C. Henley Private Investigator Quinlan McKee has returned to Los Angeles after a three-year absence, only to find herself embroiled in a world of child slavery and police corruption.

Nocturnes—JD Glass From acclaimed author, JD Glass, and featuring some of her most loved characters. Nocturnes is a collection of events and adventures, from the sensual dreamscape of the deepest love, to the brooding intensity of desire.

Bailey's Run—Ali Spooner Bailey Chambers mourns the loss of her lover, Nessa, in an unsolved carjacking. When Tommy, Bailey's brother becomes a victim of a gay bashing, Bailey assumes his case will be handled the same way as her lover's— lackadaisically.

Desi Dexter assigned to Tommy's case, feels Bailey's disdain toward her and her partner. Through tenacious police work, Desi, is able to uncover the reason for Bailey's attitude, and convinces her that she is sincere in solving the case.

Mutual attraction sparks, and before they can move forward with their fledging romance, Desi, and her partner Braxton, uncover the presence of a serial killer.

What will happen to Bailey, when, Desi, becomes engrossed in another case, can their relationship survive?

eBooks, Print, Free eBooks

Visit our website for more publications available online.

www.affinityebooks.com

Published by Affinity E-Book Press NZ LTD
Canterbury, New Zealand
Registered Company 2517228